A
KILLER
AT
LARGE

Richard Le Normand

'A Killer at Large' is a novel. The characters, situations and some of the places are entirely imaginary and bear no relation to any person, living or dead. Some of the events in this book could easily have taken place as many events happened during the Second World War which were never recorded.

The author wishes to pay his respects to the French Resistance, whose enormous efforts and great sacrifice enabled the Allies to speed up the liberation of France and so shorten the War.

Published in Australia by Temple House Pty Ltd,
T/A Sid Harta Publishers ACN 092 197 192
Hartwell, Victoria

Telephone: 61 3 9560 9920,
Facsimile: 61 3 9545 1742
E-mail: author@sidharta.com.au

First published in Australia 2005
Copyright © Richard Le Normand, 2005
Cover design, typesetting:
Chameleon Print Design

The right of Richard Le Normand to be identified as the
Author of the Work has been asserted in accordance with the
Copyright, Designs and Patents Act 1988.

Le Normand, Richard

Killer at Large
ISBN: 1-921030-81-X
pp 218

About the Author

Richard Le Normand was born in Jersey Channel Islands in 1927 and was educated at Victoria College Jersey 1936–1944. Richard left college early, to avoid being 'press-ganged' into the construction of German fortifications—most of the 'slave workers' having been killed off by then and labour was needed to complete their fortifications in Alderney, a sister isle.

After the Islands were liberated in 1945, Richard became a farmer, later specialising in intensive flower and tomato growing under glass. Richard then established a plastics factory to develop and produce new inventions, mainly in the horticultural field.

In 1987, Richard decided to retire and settle in Australia. He soon realised that retirement was not for him and became involved in marketing hydroponics. After spending nine interesting years working in real estate, Richard moved to the Gold

Coast where he developed and patented an attachment for small boats. Finally, to pay for all his past sins, Richard started to write and publish books and short stories.

Additionally, Richard has contributed three very different short stories about the random moments when we mortals lose control of time, to the anthology, *A Leap in Time*, a new literary work just published by the Carindale Writers Group. The anthology writers are all Queensland writers and the stories include fiction, non-fiction and poetry.

Acknowledgements

To dear Ruth

For all her help and support when most needed

PROLOGUE

Would it ever have occurred to you that the person sitting next to you on the ten–thirty train from Brisbane to the Gold Coast could be a cold-blooded killer? No? Well think again. The cheerful looking and ageing gentleman in the seat next to you may be just that . . .

I smiled when I looked around the carriage at the four badly behaved teenage boys and wondered if given the same circumstances they would have been able over a period of three years, to quietly and efficiently slit the throats of eight men. Could they grip and hold back a man's head whilst sliding a knife across his throat, listen to the gasp and then the gurgle as he choked to death?

Could anything arouse in them the cold and deadly anger that had given me the power to kill?

Listening to concert music that evening, the excited chatter of the young boys on their way out of the concert hall, I pondered the continual media coverage of an alleged Latvian war criminal of so long ago. Living in a country that has not had to face an enemy occupation brought back the memories.

I realised the time had finally come to tell my story, of the exploitation of sex coupled with violent death. It was getting on for sixty years since it all began and maybe now it was time to relive the experience that I had so successfully put out of my mind for so long.

Chapter One

Jersey Channel Islands 1943

Walking up the stone slipway shortly after dawn that morning, I suddenly realised I had a machine gun pointing directly at me. I stood, frozen to the spot.

I had just reached the tender age of sixteen and had slipped out of the house, two hours before curfew ended. I had gone down to the beach to look at my fishing lines, which sadly only had the remains of two red mullet.

Unfortunately, the crabs had got there first . . .

I decided to adopt the image of a silly dim teenager, which at the time I was anyway, quite unaware of the danger I had placed myself in, I gave the German guards a big smile and a happy wave and would have continued on my way. This was not to be and so began unimaginable events over which

I would have little control and which changed me from an innocent young teenager into a cold-blooded killer.

'*Halt. Kommen sie hier.*'

I was grabbed by two scruffy guards who, having finished their night duty, were unshaven and had the typical German soldier sour smell that came from living off rye bread, heavy smoking, and living in cramped conditions where showers were the exception.

Anne Port Bay, Jersey

The gun emplacement was a machine gun located on the roof of a deserted café situated across the road opposite the top of the slipway.

From this same outpost some time later, a young man was killed trying to escape from the beach in a small boat. I was marched, or rather dragged, to the back of the café and taken into the kitchen. Although I could speak a little German, I was unable to understand what the guards were shouting to me, guessing they had been drinking on duty, but I was quite unprepared for what was to come.

They started hitting me. The blows came hard and fast. I tried to shout at them to stop but my mouth was full of blood and I was beyond speech and resistance. I was pushed down onto what must have been the kitchen table and struck in the face and body. I felt my legs being pulled apart. My vision was fading. A face with a very strange expression was the last thing I remembered before I lost consciousness.

I came to later, to the sounds of a German officer screaming at the two German guards who were then led away by two *Feldgendamerie* guards. I was told later that the two soldiers had been executed without trial for sexually assaulting a civilian.

I was still lying on the kitchen table, hurting all over. My face was swollen and very sore but the agonising pain was lower down, my bottom was on fire. I felt I had been ripped apart. I slid off the table and retrieved my pants and trousers but I could not stop myself from shaking all over. At the age of sixteen I had been brutally raped.

As well as the severe pain and aching all over my body, I was overcome with a terrible feeling of shame and disbelief at what had happened to me.

That feeling of shame was to stay with me for the rest of my life and was to turn into a deep, cold and lasting anger, which was to control my actions for many years.

The German officer walked up to me and slapped my face. 'Young English piglet. You have flirted with two of my men and now they must die because of you. For that, I am arresting you on the charge of spying on the German coastal defences in this area. Piglet, you will be taken to the Gloucester Street prison in St Helier where you will be interrogated and then I hope that will be the end of you.'

I was pushed into the back of the waiting truck and wedged between two of the soldiers. Although it was a warm sunny day, I was still shaking badly. I could detect sympathetic if not warm glances from the two Germans who held onto me all the way to the prison, but the last thing I wanted to do was jump out of the truck.

At the prison, I was taken to a room where I was told to strip, given a piece of soap, and a hose was turned on me. The water was very cold but I was too upset to care. I was being treated like an animal and felt completely humiliated. I tried hard to wash away all that had happened to my body that morning, but mentally I was to feel dirty for a long time to come.

Still wet all over and naked I was marched down a flight of stairs along a narrow passageway and pushed into a small cell: no window, just a dim ceiling light, a wooden bed, blanket and bucket. The guard slapped my bare buttocks, pushing me roughly into the cell and locked the door on his way out. I lay on the bare boards of the bed, with the blanket as a pillow. Lying on my side with my legs drawn up was the most comfortable position for me, still in shock at what had happened in such a short time. My mind going around in circles, I drifted into a deep sleep.

When I woke up it must have been, I guessed, some time in the late afternoon. I had no means of telling the time with no window in my cell, it could have been night or day but I never normally slept more than seven hours at a time. I now felt really frightened. It had all happened in such a short time. I wondered if my parents knew where I was. I forced myself to calm down and think clearly about what had happened, what my position was and what I should try to do to extricate myself from this mess.

My parents had sent me to the top boys' school in Jersey, though it must have been very difficult for them. The family business was having a very hard time; the factory had been destroyed when the Germans bombed the Island. I was not a very good student, being a bit lazy, and I put more energy into enjoying myself than into my studies. However, my maths master had made a lasting impression on me and I always tried to follow his logical way of resolving problems.

In 1940, soon after the terrible events of Dunkirk and the withdrawal of the Allied forces in France, a large number of people were evacuated to Britain from the Channel Islands. At this time, the Islands received several attacks from the air in preparation for the landing of the German occupying forces. They were to remain on the Islands for the next five years. I was twelve years old at that time and although frightened during the air raids, I and the other boys found it all rather exciting. Not so our parents, who realised all the dangers and shortages we were about to experience.

The shops soon became empty. All guns, cars, motorcycles and radios were handed over to the Germans. The island was put under a permanent curfew and the currency was changed from Sterling to Reich marks. The banks were emptied and the money sent to Berlin.

Some time later when the invasion of England was called off, Hitler decided to fortify the Channel Islands, in line with the fortifications being constructed all along the French coastline. Heavy guns were brought over to the Islands to fire on any shipping entering the English Channel. To achieve this, large numbers of 'slaves' from Russia and Europe were brought to the Islands. Very many of these slaves were to die during this enormous construction of the fortifications.

Hitler was very proud to have conquered part of the United Kingdom and had special books printed for all the schoolchildren in the Islands. We were ordered to learn the German language. Although I (like all the boys at my school) tried not to learn the language, I did learn enough to be very useful in what was to happen to me in the years to come.

Starting to build the fortifications in Jersey

My first experience of slave labour came about when I, with two other boys of my age, decided to go to Fort Regent to see if we could retrieve our air pistols and which we considered quite harmless.

Inside the Fort, we happened to open a door that led into a courtyard where, to our horror, we witnessed about twenty bedraggled men running in a circle. A German with a steel whip was hitting them to make them move faster. Luckily, we had not been seen and so retreated at great speed never to go near Fort Regent again!

At another time, the boy who sat next to me at school was taken away with his father. The Germans had found them in possession of a radio set. We were told they both died in a cattle truck on the way to Germany. In those days, many stories were told of similar events.

The Gestapo were always around, their intention to create fear and therefore discipline in the civil population. It was very successful.

On thinking about my experience behind the gun emplacement and all the other events leading up to this day, my fear slowly turned to a deep and cold anger that I could feel slowly rising up inside me. It took complete control of my body and brain. In a matter of minutes, I had changed from a happy young sixteen-year-old boy into what would turn out to be a cold blooded and dangerous man. How dangerous, … I was soon to find out. A cold and calculating killer.

I realised that the German officer must have been told that I was flirting with the two Guards and had led them into thinking I was looking for a sexual encounter. Although I was ignorant of these things at the time, I did know that a few men were homosexual and did things together, but I knew I was certainly *not* like that. Girls to me were getting very interesting but as yet, in those days, quite unobtainable. I would call for a guard to bring me my clothes and take me to the officer in charge, I would explain that it was all a terrible mistake and could they ask for my parents to come and fetch me.

The cell door opened and two guards came in. They took hold of my arms. I was still naked, but they marched me along the passage and into a large bare room. An officer and an NCO were seated at a table.

The guards moved back and I was made to stand in the centre of the room on a wire mat. The two men at the table disappeared from view as the lights were switched on. The powerful lights were directed at me and I almost lost my balance trying to shield my eyes. I was now unable to see anyone else in the room. The nightmare of finding myself naked in a room full of people no longer mattered to me. I was far too worried about my situation and was past caring about my nakedness.

'Piglet is the name we have here for you. Please give us your full name.' That was the last time I was to hear the word 'please.'

I gave my full name and address and tried to explain that this was all a big mistake and that all I had done was to break curfew in order to attend to my fishing lines. I asked as politely and as calmly as I could if they would call my parents and ask them to come and collect me. I heard the sound of laughter, and the officer in charge started speaking quite softly to me.

'I think the name Piglet suits you better than your given name—a pink piglet without a tail. So we will from now on, address you as Piglet.' A short silence and then in a much stronger and sharper tone: 'It is not as simple as you would like, Piglet. Your identity card gave us your name, date of birth and address. We have informed your parents that you have been arrested for spying on our gun emplacements and that you have already been sent on to our Paris Headquarters for questioning.'

As his words sunk in, I had a deep feeling of fear and foreboding. I switched my mind to the events of that morning and felt the cold anger returning. *Yes, I liked the name Piglet. The Germans would rue the day they messed with Piglet.*

'When your mother became agitated, we warned her that you were very lucky to have been arrested by the *Wermacht* and not by the *Gestapo*. The *Gestapo* would have immediately arrested all your family, their close friends and your school friends also, Piglet. You also, Piglet, have been saved from a possible nasty slow death by the *Gestapo*—this is why you will be taken to Paris leaving the harbour three hours before dawn. You will be taken by train under escort to Paris where you will be interrogated. You will then be tried before a German Army court. At worst you will be sentenced to death, but at least it will be quick and clean.'

Then, returning to the soft but menacing voice, 'Your parents were clearly told that if they kept quiet and just told their friends that you had been taken to Paris for questioning regarding a minor offence, there would be a good chance of them seeing you again one day. However, to complain to the local authorities could lead to disaster for them and many others. Your mother and father understand the situation and will be very quiet from now on. So, Piglet, there is now just the little matter of the complaint from *Oberleutenant* Grossman. He alleges you flirted with two of his men causing them to be summarily executed for the crime of sexual assault on a member of the local population. This *flirting* is not a charge a court would handle so we will now give you a light punishment, a taste of what is to come to you when you arrive in Paris. You will raise your hands above your head.'

My hands touched what I thought was a chain to which was attached a pair of handcuffs. The chain must have been lowered down to suit my height. The two guards stepped forward. One lifted me slightly and the other clicked on the cuffs. My feet, except for my heels, were on the wire mat.

The first blow was across my bare buttocks. I nearly lost my footing. The pain was sharp and agonising. They were using a heavy cane. The second blow was on my lower legs. I let out a scream; this was to be the only one they would get from me. I had decided that anger could overcome pain so now was the time to put it to the test. It worked. As the blows rained down and the anger in my mind took over, I forgot the pain. I was planning a vicious retribution. I would kill as many Germans as I could. I would hunt down the *Oberleutenant* and I would cut his throat. He would slowly bleed to death.

The blows stopped. I had conquered pain and fear. Well, almost. I was burning all over but I had not cried, nor would I. I was dragged to the next room and was again hosed down, I did not appear to have any cuts but I knew the next day I would have many bruises over my back and legs. When they took me back to the cell, I found my clothes on the bed. By now I had become used to being naked and had lost my sense of shame. This must have been because of the defiance and anger that I had felt.

A guard reappeared with a tin of unpleasant-looking soup and a large hunk of bread. Another tin contained water. I realised how hungry and thirsty I was—I had not eaten for twenty-four hours.

'You will be shortly receiving visitor. It is now ten o'clock. In six hours you will be taken to the harbour. After visitor, you sleep.'

The food and the thought of maybe my father coming to get me out of this situation cheered me up. It came as a shock when the cell door opened and in strode *Oberleutenant* Grossman.

I had leapt up from the bed only to find myself face to face with the person who was responsible for me being in this situation. I sank back on the edge of the bed and looked up at his face. He was smiling at me. I was not sure what to expect from him. I was reminded of the expression on the face of my headmaster at prep school just before I was to receive a heavy caning.

'So, my Piglet, you have a sore arse, huh? That is good, a small compensation for me. However, you have stirred up certain feelings within me, which, I have decided, will make me more lenient towards you. I also will travel to Paris. I travel on behalf of the prosecution; I hold your life in my hands. On the other hand, for certain small favours . . . I could help you.'

I was shocked, but then it all fell into place. This Grossman was a homosexual and he was going to take control of me. My mind was racing: do I go along with this and then go back to face my family, or was I prepared to face more beatings and then finally be executed?

I knew that if I did what this swine expected, I could never go back to my family without feeling a terrible shame that would be with me forever. I could not face that.

My eyes were about level with his waist. I looked at his

revolver and wondered if I could snatch it from its holster. Impossible.

Then it dawned on me that maybe Grossman had handed me a different and perhaps, very powerful weapon that I could use to my advantage, but not at this moment.

I decided to take a risk.

I looked up at his face with an innocent smile, '*Herr Oberleutenant*, what am I expected to do and how are you able to help me?'

Grossman roared with laughter, turned on his heel and walked out of the cell. I was puzzled at first and then on reflection began to feel rather stupid.

The *Oberleutenant* called the guard as he left the cell, the guard looked back and smiled.

Within minutes, I was fast asleep.

Chapter Two

'Wake up Piglet.' The guard was leaning over me. It took several seconds for me to realise where I was. 'We leave in ten minutes.' He had placed a tin of liquid porridge and a tin of water by the door and on the bed—a grubby looking jacket. I was still dressed in my fishing clothes—just shirt, pants and trousers so the jacket was very welcome to me at this time of night.

I washed my face with some of the water and ate the porridge, or rather drank it and painfully moved around the room until I was able to rid myself of the stiffness from the beating of the evening before.

Two guards came in and I was marched out of the cell along the passages and out through the large studded door of the prison. It was pitch dark and quite cold. We walked the length of the esplanade and then all the way down to the end of the jetty past several converted river barges that were used to bring troops, slaves and supplies to the island. We went down a steep gangway onto the deck of a German patrol boat.

This rather surprised me as I expected to be taken to France on one of those converted barges. I realised the reason for the patrol boat was that neither the Army nor the Navy wanted the *Gestapo* involved in my arrest.

Long and deep investigation by the *Gestapo* often revealed matters that also involved members of the armed services and so for their own sakes they were determined to get me to their Paris headquarters as quietly and as quickly as possible.

Not being a good sailor, I was pleased that we were travelling on a fast and therefore a much safer boat across the thirty-odd miles of water to France. Maybe we would get to our destination before daylight and avoid being attacked from the air.

The walled city of St Malo

We were taken to the stern of the boat where I was then handcuffed to one of the guards. I carefully noted into which pocket he put the key.

The other guard laughed and saluted his friend. 'Some people get all the luck; have a good time in Paris.' He turned on his heel and marched up the gangway and into the night.

We sat on a pile of rope between the depth charges and I wondered what would happen if they decided to fire them. When I asked, the time by the guard's watch (stolen I expect from some unfortunate prisoner) was three-thirty am.

Although the deep anger was still with me, because of my age I expect, I had a slight feeling of excitement and adventure and my spirits lifted a little. It was time to plan how I was going to escape. I had no intention of going to Paris and perhaps face a firing squad. If I was going to die, it would be at *my* time and place and I would try to take a German with me. Such is the optimism of youth.

I knew we had a choice of two ports: St Malo or Granville. Granville was the nearest and had a better train link with Paris. However, we went to St Malo, it took us five hours. That suited the plan that was starting to form in my mind. My father had mentioned at some time, that it used to be a slow train from St Servant to Rennes via Dol, where you then changed to a faster train for Paris.

However, that was before the war so things might have changed a lot since then. Grossman had given me a very useful tool that I intended to use on the guard and which would give me a good opportunity to escape—sex.

The guard's name was Heinrig. Henry was of medium height, a little on the fat side and to me quite old, at least thirty. He came from Austria and was married. I noticed he kept looking down at me and when he accidentally brushed his hand against my leg, I looked up and smiled at him. I had started the process that could lead to my escape. Henry did not have a heavy coat or helmet. He carried a light bag and was armed with a revolver and a bayonet. It was this that interested me, not the revolver. I had a plan that would depend mainly on the time that we left St Malo for Paris, for I would need the cover of darkness to make my plan work.

A sailor appeared with two mugs of *ersatz* coffee and two large hunks of bread filled with a very tasty sausage a real 'hot dog'. This was the best food I had tasted for a long time and was also the last good food I was to get for quite some time.

We left Jersey at low tide so that we could enter the St Malo basin at high tide and avoid using the damaged lock gates. As it took five hours to reach St Malo, we must have gone the long way around the large reef that ran between Jersey and St Malo. It was a bright sunny day when we arrived and we had not been attacked by Allied planes. Several barges carrying supplies to the islands had been sunk recently including food for the civilian population. There was a whole lot of activity on the dockside.

Barges were being loaded for the Channel Islands with food for the local and German population, guns and ammunition. The islands were not liberated until well after the French ports were retaken by the Americans, which meant the Germans were cut off from their supplies and were facing starvation by the time the war ended. The civilian population by then were receiving Red Cross parcels.

The lock gates to the harbour basin had been badly damaged when the British forces had evacuated in 1940, but they had been repaired sufficiently for us to enter the basin and tie up close to the old city wall. St Malo was a very fine walled-in city and was later to be flattened by the Americans. After the war, St Malo, with the aid of America, was restored stone by stone.

We disembarked, crossed the road and entered the old city through an archway. Henry marched me to an office which was a converted bar in the old city wall, a part that later survived the bombing that destroyed the town. The handcuffs were removed and I was told to sit on a bench whilst my guard completed all the paperwork and was given the train passes.

An entrance into St Malo

Our train was to leave St Servan at eleven am; it was now nine-thirty am.

We were told we would have to walk to the station at St Servan, which was, I think, about two miles from where we were. I liked the idea of walking as I needed the exercise both for body and mind. The handcuffs had been put back on so I was securely attached to Henry. I think he liked having me attached to him.

I was a bit disappointed that the train was leaving so early, as my plan would have a better chance of success after dark and that meant delaying my move until we were almost in Paris. But I was about to get a little help from above.

We were about halfway to the station, in open ground with the water on one side and wooden sheds on the other. It looked like a holding place for slave workers. We heard the sound of aeroplane engines, which quickly turned to a roar. Henry pulled me down into a ditch that was filled with filthy water and then all hell was let loose as three *Spitfires* skimmed overhead, followed by the roar of exploding bombs.

In the silence that followed this lightening attack, we picked ourselves up, soaked from the very dirty water we had fallen into, but otherwise both unharmed. We could see a cloud of black smoke rising from the station, when we got there the train was no more. The engine and two carriages had been destroyed and First Aid workers and police were pulling out the dead and wounded. This was my first experience of death at close range. Forty-eight hours ago I would have been shocked, instead I found myself smiling. This was not the innocent boy of yesterday. I was now a man and was soon to be a vicious killer.

We eventually found the Station Master who directed us to a truck that was going to Dol where we were then to get a train to Rennes if the lines were open. The journey to Dol was very uncomfortable. The road must have been damaged in several places by the Allied bombing and at times it felt as if we were not even on the road it was so bumpy. Henry had undone the handcuffs so that we could keep our balance, as the truck had to swing from side to side in order to dodge the worst of the damaged road. We were one of several armed trucks, I presumed because of possible attack from the French Resistance. Safety in numbers, but I just hoped we would not be strafed by another RAF patrol, it would be a shame to be killed that way and by our own side.

The railway yards were very busy at Dol as this was the crossroads to Mont St Michel, Granville and Cherbourg to the East and North, whilst to the West, St Malo, Dinan, St Brieuc, Morlaix and Brest.

The damage from bombing was everywhere but despite the Allied bombing, there was still a lot of activity transferring supplies from railway trucks to a string of waiting army trucks. I guessed most of the train movements must have taken place at night. I did notice that the trucks were being loaded and unloaded by slave workers heavenly guarded by armed soldiers.

Henry clicked on the handcuffs and we both carefully lowered ourselves from the truck. It was now one forty-five pm according to an ancient railway clock on the departure platform. We entered the cigarette smoke-filled Army Station Master's office and an officer told Henry that we would board a train that was passing through at seven that evening or thereabouts. We were to report to his office at six-thirty. In the meantime, he gave us an address in the town where friendly locals and collaborators would feed us and we would be able to rest there until it was time to return to the station.

Henry was on no account to release me from the handcuffs and he was told that he was entirely responsible for my safe delivery to the headquarters in Paris.

The Railway Bridge

We found the café, which was down a side street just off the main square; we went down two steps into a dingy room with lots of wooden tables and benches. There were several soldiers and Navy men sitting around eating and drinking, all I presume waiting for trains that were going in different directions that evening.

The *patron* was expecting us and we were taken to a small room up some stairs. It had a table, chairs and a bed. There was no door to the room and just a very small window. The *patron* returned with two bowls of vegetable soup, a camembert cheese, tomatoes, an onion and a small loaf of German rye bread. This to me was an absolute feast. He returned a few minutes later with a bottle of local cider, a carafe of water and two grimy glasses. Henry slipped two English pound notes, stolen in Jersey no doubt, into the *patron's* pocket. He must have been here before. Between us we polished off all the food, but one taste of the cider was enough for me, I stuck to the water. I would need a very clear head for the next few hours.

We moved across to the bed, still handcuffed and lay alongside each other. Henry's free hand came across and touched my thigh. I gave him a sweet, innocent smile and luckily for me, the cider took affect. Henry fell asleep.

I had made this train journey five years ago with my dad; it was about thirty-four miles from Dol to Rennes, between the villages of Comburg and St Germain and a little before St Germain, there were two bridges fairly close together in wooded countryside. This would be the best place to jump. Hopefully the train would stop at some of these small stations or would be slow enough for me to at least see their names. I had a vague idea of how to deal with Henry. He was a substantially built man and I felt sure that he must be very fit.

I was certainly not strong enough to overpower a person like him; I would have to be very agile, cunning and fast moving.

We arrived back at the Station Master's office sharp at six-thirty and were directed to a waiting room where there were a number of other people—civilians, army and navy personnel. At seven forty-five our train arrived, two passenger carriages and a whole string of goods wagons. We were escorted to the rear of the second carriage by the Station Master's assistant. I had the window seat on the right hand side, which was to prove very useful when it came to making my move.

The carriage was about half-full and once we got under way, I noticed that most of the passengers were either sleeping or looking as if they would be asleep soon. Being late summer, the days were still quite long. It was after eight by Henry's watch and the light was beginning to fade. Another hour and it would be dark.

The train was moving very slowly, I thought about fifteen miles per hour, a good running speed. If Rennes was thirty-four miles, then I reckoned that it would be about a two and a half hour journey and I should therefore be ready to move just after nine—by Henry's watch in about forty-five minute's time.

Henry had been a bit quiet since leaving the café, I think it must have been the effects of the cider so I moved our attached hands between his legs and wriggled up closer to him, when he looked down at me I gave him my sweet innocent smile. I would exploit the situation. I had a feeling of excitement, fear, and deep anger as I thought of my rape by the two guards. I continued to tease this German; it was going to be his last bit of pleasure in life.

We halted at Comburg and two civilians got off the train. Our next stop was Montreuil where just one person left the train. Time to move; it was getting pretty dark and we were moving through what appeared to be woodland.

'Henry, I badly need to go to the toilet.'

I gave him my warmest smile. 'Will you take me?' I held his hand.

He got the meaning and started to move. Out of the window I could see water; we were travelling alongside the Rance which ran from St Malo to Rennes. Perfect.

Where Marçel jumped the train

The toilet was very close to us at the rear of the carriage. We squashed in and Henry locked the door. He took off the handcuffs and laid his belt with his revolver and bayonet on the toilet seat.

Henry sank to his knees and lowered my trousers. What he did next roused me from my anger to a cold and clear-minded rage . . .

I slowly withdrew his bayonet and with a hand at each end, I brought it down with all my strength to the back of his neck. Henry collapsed in a heap. I think he was already dead but I held back his head and slashed his throat to make sure. The train rattled as it crossed the second bridge.

Henry was dead.

There was blood everywhere. I picked up the bayonet and wiped it on Henry's jacket. I removed his watch, placed the revolver and bayonet in his shoulder bag, pulled his body to one side of the toilet and with his bag over my arm, slowly opened the door. All was clear.

I crossed to the carriage door and looking out of the window, saw that the moon had come out. We were travelling alongside the Rance. The railway line was very near the riverbank, which was covered with grass and tall weeds. Perfect.

I opened the door and clutching the bag, leapt out as far as I could from the train. I hit the bank hard and allowed myself to keep rolling until I fell into in the water. I scrambled back onto the bank, removed my shoes and jacket and squeezed them into the bag. The river, which was really a canal, was not very wide and I was a very good swimmer. I re-entered the water and lying on my back holding the bag with one hand, managed to slowly make my way across the canal.

I reached the bank on the opposite side, climbed out of the water, crossed the footpath and moved into the woodland. I found a spot amongst some bushes and sat down.

It was time to savour my escape and assess my situation.

I felt bruised and battered but was otherwise quite intact, except for a light cut on my left hand from holding the bayonet at both ends when I delivered my first blow to Henry. The rage had subsided and I was elated at what I had achieved, I felt no remorse or horror at what I had done—Henry had got what he deserved. I had killed my first German and it had been easy. Now there were three dead because of me in two days. Not bad.

So my position was this: Henry's body would be discovered at Rennes, or before if someone used the toilet, but I had all the documents regarding my arrest so it would take some time for the authorities to know who to look for and where to start looking. They may not even bother to do that, as so many Germans were being killed by the Resistance at this time and it might be simpler to just cover up the loss of one more soldier. However, I knew that I had to get as far away as possible away from this railway line. I decided to become absorbed into the French way of life, perhaps on a farm, and keep a very low profile until the end of the war when I could return to Jersey.

Fate was to decide otherwise . . .

Chapter Three

I decided to move on and find a place where I could dispose of the documents, the shoulder bag and all traces of Henry. I moved on through the woods up a steep slope, along a ridge and down a grass field to a road that I followed, keeping well to the side in case I had to dive for cover if any Germans were to appear.

I realised I would need certain things if I was going to survive—food, a map, a compass, a strong pair of shoes, I would also need some kind of bag as I could not, for obvious reasons, keep Henry's bag.

I noticed a large pond a little way off the road so went across to look at it. At one end of the pond there was a dilapidated hut surrounded by reeds, no doubt used for duck shooting. Inside the hut, I placed Henry's bag on a bench.

The first thing I found in the bag was a small flat German army torch, two boxes of matches, four packets of cigarettes of no use to me but they could be used perhaps as currency for food. There was a bag of toilet things, (I might find the razor useful later to shave the few whiskers that were starting to grow on my face) a grubby pair of underpants and a vest. Henry did not intend to stay long in Paris I guessed. There were several documents that referred to me, including the passes to take us to our destination. These I burnt using Henry's matches and I hid the ashes amongst the reeds. To my delight at the bottom of the bag I found a small army compass, this was the best thing that I found in the bag and was to prove very useful to me in the future.

Henry's toilet bag was quite big. It was a cloth bag that had a strong tape for closing it up. I expect Henry's wife must have made it for him. I put the razor, toothpaste, soap, cigarettes, matches and torch back into the toilet bag. After washing off the blood, I attached the bayonet to my belt and slipped it on the inside of my trousers. This was a bit uncomfortable but necessary. The compass I kept in my pocket. The rest of the things, including the revolver, I put in Henry's bag. I found a large stone which I also put in the bag and then waded into the pond up to my waist and lowered Henry's bag deep into the mud. I checked to see if I had left anything in the hut and clutching Henry's toilet bag walked back to the road.

Although the sky was now overcast, it was still light enough for me to see where I was going. According to the compass, the road was heading north. I found myself once again following the canal; I kept well clear of a series of locks, which must have been close to Hédé. Several hours later, I passed some houses and a battered sign by the side of the road that said 'Tinteniac'.

I walked cautiously along the village street past a few shops, but there were no locals about as it was long past curfew. There were a few cottages on the far side of the village.

I suddenly froze.

Just a few yards in front of me, I could see a German guard, he was standing on a stone bridge, lighting a cigarette.

I sank down to my hands and knees and slowly backed away, slipping into some low bushes. I was in the garden of the last cottage. Two motorcycles with sidecars were parked outside. The Germans who were guarding the bridge must have been based there. I kept slowly moving backwards until I came up against a low fence, slipped over the fence and landed in a duck's pen. I decided to get to the back of the cottages where there must be better cover.

I found a lane that ran behind the cottages. At the end of the lane there was a narrow river, and close by, a smart looking house with a large garden in front. At the side of the house was a double garage. This would be my target, hopefully I would get an opportunity to get inside, steal some food and perhaps find some more suitable clothes.

I found a small unlocked shed in the garden that was almost hidden by an overgrown magnolia bush from which I was able to clearly see the front of the house. I lay down on the bare boards inside the shed and fell asleep, oblivious to the sound of an arriving motor cycle, the slamming of a garage door and the opening and closing of the front door.

The sound of dogs barking woke me up. The front door of the house was open; two small dogs were dashing around the garden, chased by an attractive woman in a dressing gown.

After a while, the woman and the dogs disappeared into the house and the door closed.

It was a fine summer day and it would soon become very warm inside the shed. I was hungry and thirsty but I was going to have to wait until the house was empty before I could leave the shed. I would have to reconsider my plan if the people remained in the house. It was more than likely that on a lovely summer's day like this the house would be unoccupied for a short while at least and I would be able to slip in and steal what I needed.

I looked at Henry's watch, seven-thirty am.

An hour later, a man came out of the front door. He was well dressed and wearing a dark suit and carried a large briefcase. He crossed to the garage and backed out a small Renault motor car. The woman, also smartly dressed, followed by the two dogs and carrying a small suitcase, came out of the house slamming the door behind her. She ran across the garden to the waiting car. The dogs scrambled into the back of the car and the woman got into the front. The car turned on the gravel driveway and travelling fast, disappeared up the lane.

At least my problem with the dogs was solved. I moved over to the house, which had French windows either side of the front door.

I decided to explore the back of the house first as it might have an open window, also I might have to make a quick getaway if the owners returned. More French windows opened onto a large lawn that had several laden apple trees. At the far end of the lawn I could see a vegetable garden and behind that, the river with trees growing right down to the water on both sides. I thought I would leave that way, crossing the river into the woodland that would provide cover for me all the way to the hillside, which I could see in the distance.

The kitchen door was at the far end of the house close to the garage. Using the bayonet, I forced open the door and entered the passageway that led into the kitchen. On one side of the passage, there was a washing machine and several cupboards, on the other side a row of hooks with waterproof jackets and raincoats, underneath a row of boots and shoes. I spotted a dark green backpack under one of the jackets. This was perfect; I took it down and carried it into the kitchen. It was a large bright kitchen with a solid table and chairs in the middle. I went straight to the fridge and found to my delight a jug of milk and some pastries that I quickly devoured. I filled the bag with bread, cheese, a large piece of ham and a few tomatoes. I also found a large unopened packet of biscuits and a bottle of mineral water; this almost filled the backpack. I selected a sharp medium-sized kitchen knife and slipped it into the bag. The kitchen dresser had several books and magazines and there among the books I found a Michelin road map that I slipped into the bag with a plate, cup, some cutlery and a small saucepan. This was all I could fit in to the backpack.

I left the bag on the table and went through to the dining room, which had some fine Breton carved furniture. I noticed several silver framed photos, one of which was a group of German officers and civilians.

I should have taken more notice of this . . .

At the top of the stairs there were four doors. I walked through one that was open and which happened to be the main bedroom. It was a lovely room with fine dark wood furniture and brightly coloured bed covers. The owners of this home had good taste and must have been wealthy so I guessed they would not miss one or two modest items. I started to look at the man's clothes in the walk-in wardrobe, they were all much too large for me but I found a pair of strong walking shoes and was packing the toes with socks so that they would fit me, when I received a blow to my head.

I opened my eyes some time later; a familiar face was staring down at me.

'So, Piglet, we meet again.'

It took me several seconds to realise I was looking up at the smiling face of *Oberleutenant* Grossman.

'How strange you should have found yourself at my sister's house tucked away in the middle of the French countryside. Fate has decided that we should meet again.'

He was smiling down at me but I seemed to detect a slight change in his appearance; he looked far less arrogant.

I was tied to a small bed with my hands and legs tightly fastened with leather bootlaces. There was a large bed on the other side of the room and I noticed Grossman's hat and jacket on an armchair and an open case on the floor. This must be his bedroom. How did he get here, how on earth did he find me? I wondered what sort of treatment I would receive after my last encounter with him.

'I could not have imagined the chaos that would arise from your arrest, what I thought was an over-sexed young local boy has turned out to be something quite different. That innocent smiling boy turned out to be a young psychopath. I completely misjudged you, Piglet. That you should calmly accept the beating in prison and then go on to commit the savage murder of one of our men is not what I would have expected from a normal teenage boy.'

Grossman crossed the room and moving his hat and jacket, sat in the armchair staring at me for several minutes.

'Your score so far: three German soldiers dead and thanks to you, one German Army officer now on the run. All this in forty-eight hours; not bad for a sixteen-year-old.'

Grossman paused to light himself a cigarette. He seemed very calm and quite different to the person that had visited me in my cell after my beating.

'As stated before, Piglet, I find it quite extraordinary that you should turn up here at my sister's home,' he continued. 'The guard found the soldier's body on the train on which I also was travelling, I did not realise at the time that your train had been destroyed at St.Servan and that you were on the same train as me. After the discovery of the body, the train was diverted to a siding at Renne; the *Gestapo* arrived and took charge. Everyone on the train was interrogated. They must have contacted headquarters in Jersey, because by the time they got to me they knew all about your case, my involvement as arresting officer and even my visit to you in prison. I knew by then they had figured out that I was somehow involved in the murder and with your disappearance.'

Grossman paced the room, and finally looked down at me and slowly continued, 'We were all allowed to leave the train. It was well after midnight but I was told to report to the Renne *Gestapo* headquarters at ten am. I knew that I was already under suspicion by the *Gestapo*. They had found out that I had a sister somewhere in France and that her husband was known to be sympathetic to the Allies. I realised that now they would make every effort to track her down and use her to break me.' Grossman returned to the chair and lit another cigarette.

'After the *Gestapo* left I walked across to the Army depot, as an Army officer I had no problem in commandeering a motorcycle. It took me less than two hours to get here to warn Gerda and her husband Pierre of their danger. Pierre is a well-known lawyer with contacts all over France. They will drive to the south where their friends in the Maque will guide them across the Pyrenees and into Spain where they should be safe for the rest of the war. So, my little Piglet, we are now both in deep trouble.'

If Grossman was looking for sympathy then he was mistaken—I was getting a great deal of pleasure from his predicament, I waited for him to continue.

'Anytime now the *Gestapo* will arrive here and we will both be arrested and I have no doubt that we will, for different reasons, both die. I have two options—if I run I will probably be picked up by the Resistance and they will show no mercy towards an officer of the *Wermacht*. I'm sure it will not be a pleasant death. Unlike my brother-in-law, I do not have any contacts in France and I would have very little chance of reaching Spain.' Grossman paused for a moment.

'My other option is to surrender myself to the *Gestapo* and face disgrace and probably be executed for murder and treason. Some choice!' Grossman seemed lost in thought for some time. I remained silent. At last he came over and looked down at me still tied up and lying on the bed. I was beginning to lose the feeling in my wrists and ankles and also needed to relieve myself.

'For you, little Piglet, the situation is slightly different. I must admit I admire your resourcefulness, to have gone so far. But for the sheer coincidence and your bad luck in finding me here, you would have been well on your way by now. Piglet you still stand a very good chance of saving yourself. I know the locals would help you to hide and you would probably eventually get to England.'

The *Oberleutenant* picked up his revolver, clicked back the safety catch and pointed it at my head.

I closed my eyes and allowed my anger to take over.

I would not cry out.

Instead, I wet my trousers.

'I shall play a little game with you, Piglet. You must have, like me, played the game of hide-and-seek when you were a child. I shall untie you and I will count to thirty and then come after you. If I find you after that, I will kill you. I shall be interested to see how fast you can run. If you get away from me, maybe when the war is over you might return to this house and meet my sister.'

Still pointing the revolver at me, with one hand Grossman untied the bootlaces. He moved back and sat in the chair. I rubbed my wrists and ankles and stood up.

I noticed a slight smile on his face. 'Good luck, little Piglet. *Ein, zwie, drie . . .*'

I turned and ran down the stairs and into the kitchen. The backpack was still on the table; I grabbed it and flew out into the back garden. I was halfway across the lawn when I heard a gunshot, I stopped dead. I had to go back, I walked slowly back to the house, through the kitchen and up the stairs.

Grossman was still sitting in the armchair—dead.

I was about to relieve him of his wallet and revolver, but it occurred to me that when the *Gestapo* arrived and found Grossman had been killed and robbed, they might guess it was me and the whole area would be searched until I was found.

I retrieved the bootlaces and tidied the bed where I had been tied up and left Grossman still clutching his revolver.

On the way downstairs, I slipped on the shoes I had been looking at when I had been hit on the head. I was careful not to leave any traces of my visit in the kitchen. Leaving the backpack outside, I covered with mud the marks on the door that I had made when I opened it with the bayonet. I locked the door from the inside again being careful to leave everything undisturbed. I slipped out of the kitchen window, closing it behind me.

Picking up the backpack, I walked slowly back across the grass to the river and waded downstream for some time before crossing and climbing up the opposite bank.

I very soon disappeared into the woods.

Converted barges on the Rance

Chapter Four

With no one in sight, I crossed a main road that happened to be the main road from Renne to St Malo. I found a track that took me through the forest shaded from the afternoon sun by tall trees. The track wound its way up the side of the hill and I soon reached the top. I had been walking for about forty-five minutes when I decided to have a rest.

I found a clearing a little way off the track and right on top of the ridge. From there I had a wonderful view of the countryside both to the north and to the south. France on a warm summer's day was really quite something. It was hard to believe that there was a war going on.

I had come from the southeast and behind me I could see the house that I had just left with the stream at the bottom of the garden. The stream joined the river, which then curved around to the west where it disappeared behind the hill where I stood. The village behind the house was quite small, a stone bridge crossed the stream at the end of the village where I had seen the guard the night before and which was some way beyond the house. In the distance behind the village, I could see the main river and a much larger village with a series of locks and the lockkeeper's house close by. I could just see two barges passing through them; I expected that they were carrying German supplies.

Looking to the north I saw the river reappearing from behind the hill, the road I had just crossed ran through another small village to a bridge that crossed the main river. The road continued to the north until it disappeared from sight. The river flowed to the west, then curved again quite sharply and disappeared to the north where it eventually finished up at St Malo and the open sea.

On the bend to the north, there was a branch that ran to the southwest for about four miles, it then became a large area of high reeds. Amongst the reeds I spotted what looked like a small shed.

I decided I would go there as it would certainly be out of sight from a lower level and might make a suitable shelter for me.

An hour later, I arrived at the spot where I had seen the shed.

I walked around the reeds until I found a muddy path that took me to the water's edge. I waded through the reeds and when I got to some open water, to my surprise, I found three derelict river barges. By the time I reached them I was up to my waist in water but managed to climb up the side of the nearest one.

The barges were very badly damaged and two of them had been burnt out completely—victims of allied bombing. They were tied together and seemed firmly stuck on the riverbed so I could step from one to the other. They must have been towed to this spot and then flooded. The third boat had the bow completely wrecked; it looked as if the back was broken as both bow and stern were lower than the middle section. The bridge and stern accommodation of this barge appeared to be undamaged. This was the 'shed' I had seen from the top of the hill. All the glass had been blown out of the bridge section. I entered through a door that was still intact; the inside had been stripped of all fittings including the steering wheel. A broken door led down two steps to the living area, which had also been stripped of everything except for a large wooden table in the centre. On one side of the cabin was an iron stove with a chimney that went out through the roof. The portholes still had glass in them, and set in to both of the side walls of the cabin were four bunks.

At the rear end of the cabin, steps led up to the stern deck and another set of steps led down into the engine room. Although there was some water, I could see the engine and all the controls had been removed so I closed the hatch that led down to that section and climbed up onto the rear deck.

It was a lovely summer evening and I was standing on the small deck of my new home, all around me were tall reeds and water. This was an ideal hiding place, unlikely to be visited by anyone. I could easily escape into the reeds if any Germans were to appear and there would be no give-away footprints around the barge to show that I was living here.

I sat on the roof of the cabin and ate some of the food I had stolen, pleased that I had brought the bottle of water as I did not fancy drinking unboiled water from the lake.

On reflection, I realised I could not return to Jersey until the war was over and even then, I could not imagine having to go back and explain to my parents the events that had happened to me in the last few days. So I decided I would start a new life, I now had a home. I would try to make contact with the French Resistance Movement and in the meantime, I would start my own little war with Germany. First I would have to get myself very fit. That would mean good food and some hard training. I would start right now. It was at this point that I decided to change my name to Marçel Beaumont.

After a good rest I packed the contents of the backpack into one of the several cupboards in the living room, tucked the bayonet into my trousers and wearing the empty backpack, set off back to the house. It had taken me three hours to get here so it should take two and a half hours to get back. If the house was still empty I would collect some bedding and as much food as I could carry.

The journey back was easy; I used the compass to take bearings to help me find my way back to the barges. It was quite dark when I arrived at the stream. I took off my shoes and stripped down to my pants and swam across to the garden. In my bare feet, I crept slowly up to the house. No lights were visible so I circled the house. There was no sign of life and no vehicles parked outside. I entered the garage from the side door and shone Henry's torch around.

There was very little in the garage. A bench at one end with tools neatly fastened to the wall and in one corner all the gardening tools including a lawn mower. I flashed the torch upwards and to my delight, I saw an Indian-type canoe suspended from the rafters. I managed to lower it down to the floor. It had two paddles inside and looked in very good condition. I put an assortment of tools, nails and a length of rope inside and very carefully dragged it down to the water's edge making sure not to leave any tracks behind.

Returning to the house, I was able to enter by the same kitchen window that I had used earlier that afternoon. The kitchen was in a mess; all the cupboards and drawers had been emptied but the food, to my surprise, was still there. In the dining room the same thing, I noticed the photos and all the silver had been taken. Upstairs, Grossman had been removed and apart from bloodstains on the armchair, there was no sign of his having been in the house.

Amongst the chaos in the main bedroom, I spread out a sheet onto which I piled an assortment of bedding. I found a pair of Gerda's slacks that fitted me quite well so I put them onto the pile along with one of her sweaters, adding two towels and some of Pierre's socks and underpants.

I pulled the four corners of the sheet together and tied them in a knot; it now looked like a very large Christmas pudding, which fitted nicely into the centre of the canoe. Going back to the kitchen I loaded all the food I could find into the backpack, closed the kitchen door and returned to the canoe, which I slid into the water, climbed into the rear end and paddled across to where I had left my clothes.

This, I thought, was the start of another great adventure.

With the tools and bedding in the bow end, the canoe was well balanced and slid nicely through the water. I reckoned after joining the main river I should arrive at the turning point, where the barges were, by dawn—say five hours. I then remembered I had to pass under the stone bridge that was guarded by a German soldier and later, the larger road bridge crossing the main river.

I pulled into the bank on the opposite side of the stream and spent a few minutes thinking how I could get rid of the guard. Just to slit his throat and leave him would alert the *Gestapo* that I was in this area and so a search would probably reveal my new home. A plan was forming in my mind, which was again going to entail some very good timing and a lot of luck.

I moved slowly to the bridge and crouched below the end of the bridge wall. I could see the guard at the other end of the bridge leaning on it, smoking. I slipped out and placed Henry's torch upside down three feet beyond the end of the wall. When I turned it on, it gave just a glimmer of light. I slipped back behind the wall and started throwing stones as far as I could down the track from the bridge. The guard heard the noise and moved slowly across the bridge. I stopped throwing the stones. He walked past me on the other side of the wall and noticed the faint light on the road. As he bent down to look at the torch, I stepped forward and with the bayonet held with both hands above my head, brought it down across the back of his neck just below his helmet. It was instant death.

I picked up the torch and ran back to the canoe, paddled under the bridge and twenty yards past the bridge, I jumped back onto the bank and ran back to the guard. He had four hand grenades attached to his belt; I pulled out the pins on two of them and ran as fast as I could back to the canoe.

I had barely made it when the grenades went off. I leaped into the canoe and paddled like mad until I reached the main river, now I was well out of sight. Hopefully the other guards would assume this German had taken his own life. I felt strangely elated. I had just enjoyed another killing . . .

I paddled on for the next four hours keeping close to the riverbank. It was just beginning to get light when I spotted the road bridge. I waited until I heard some trucks approaching the bridge, then keeping close to the river bank, quietly slipped past. The guards were watching the trucks. I was very lucky. I reached the entrance to the turnoff where the barges were. If I had not known it was there, I could easily have gone straight past—another good reason for making it my home.

I tied up the canoe at the stern end of my barge, keeping it well under the stern and between the two barges; it was almost out of sight. I carried the Christmas pudding down the hatch and dropped it on the floor.

It was then the gun went off. I threw myself onto the Christmas pudding—I had not been hit.

'Stand up slowly, dear boy, with your hands above your head.' An English voice—who the hell was this? I was shocked. He had tried to kill me. 'Now slowly turn around and keep your hands up.'

I turned to see two faces peering over the engine room hatch and a revolver pointing straight at me.

'*Bonjour mon petit cochon, quel méchant voleur.*' A man with a pencil-line moustache stepped out and checked to see if I had a gun. He was admiring my bloodstained bayonet when the other man came across and dropped his gun on the table.

'Just testing your reaction, dear boy, you will have to learn to move faster than that if you want to survive around here. My name is Pete and my friend here is Pierre, easy to remember, and you, dear boy, I gather are the famous "Piglet".'

Pete smiled at me, 'Pierre has a bone or two to pick with you, killing his brother-in-law and robbing his house. Naughty boy.'

'I thought Pierre had gone to Spain with his wife, I don't understand what is going on. What are you doing here?' I was still recovering from the gunshot and was confused at the sudden appearance of the two men.

Pierre looked down at me; he was no longer wearing his smart suit, just open shirt and trousers.

'What have you stolen from me this time, Piglet?' his English was perfect. 'Did you enjoy killing my wife's brother?' I noticed he was also smiling and did not seem to be too bothered about his brother-in-law's death.

'The *Oberleutenant* took his own life after letting me escape. He also told me that you and your wife Gerda had gone to Spain.'

'Yes, Gerda has gone to Spain but Pete decided that I had work to do here. Klaus, my brother-in-law, told us all about you and how you had got him into so much trouble. He had no alternative but to do what he did. It would have come to that sooner or later anyway. He knew too much about our involvement with the Resistance and would have cracked under *Gestapo* questioning. Klaus even suggested you might be of some use to us. I am very sorry, he was a good man caught up in an impossible situation.'

Pete gave me a friendly punch in the chest. 'There ain't much of you there, young Piglet. We have followed your every move since you first left Pierre's house. We followed you here and we followed you back to the house. We saw how you dealt with the guard. I must say I was most impressed the way you pulled out the pins of the hand grenades to cover your tracks.' He paused. 'I don't suppose you brought any wine from the house, Piglet?'

'I'm afraid not, I don't drink myself but I like to see Germans drink. It makes them more vulnerable and easier to kill.'

'So far, Piglet, you have passed all the tests. We believe you might be of some use to us, King and country and all that. You seem to be quite good at killing Germans, but that is only a small part of what we do. Gathering information is our primary aim. Because of your size, your ability to improvise and kill when necessary, you could be very useful to us. There is no glory in what we do; we are the lowest of the low and very dispensable.'

Pete grabbed me by the shoulders. His face was almost touching mine and he seemed to be searching my soul. I saw so much power in his eyes: I knew then that I would walk through fire for this man.

'When any one of our people are taken by the *Gestapo*, they are tortured until they divulge all they know. Afterwards the *Gestapo* kill off what little life is left in them. So if you join our little party, you will only be told about the jobs you do. You will have no direct contact with anyone except Pierre. So, dear boy, are you with us or not?'

I remained silent for several moments.

'Do I get paid?'

They both laughed, 'Definitely NO. You will be supplied

with the tools of the trade and possibly an allowance to purchase food but only at specified times and places.'

'I had already decided to start my new life here and to devote my time to killing Germans. It would seem I would be able to kill a lot more by working with you. So I'm with you all the way!'

'A wise decision, dear boy. By the way, we would have killed you if you had said no. So let's have some of Pierre's food and later when it gets dusk, you can take us for a ride in your new canoe. I hate getting my feet wet.'

We unloaded the canoe and sat on the cabin roof eating tinned asparagus, sardines and rather stale bread. We shared the last of the water.

'I'm returning to London soon. You must forget you have ever seen me. Pierre will keep in contact with you. Remember if you are caught you know no one and we certainly will not be able give you any help. Find a good hiding spot on the barge and put everything there when you are away for any time. Today you will have learned to check very carefully before coming back on board.'

Pete handed me a small pad and pencil. 'I want you to get yourself very fit, especially when using the canoe. One day you might need to travel far and fast; in the meantime your job is to watch the railway bridges. We want to know the times and number of trains passing these bridges at night.'

'Don't try to kill too many guards! If you do, make sure you safely dispose of the bodies, too many missing guards in this area will lead to widespread searches and one day you will be caught.'

We cleaned out the bunks, shared the bedding and rested

until dusk. I paddled my passengers through the reeds to the bank of the river. Pierre shook my hand.

'I will bring you food in two days time; find yourself a stream with fresh water. And no fires at any time.'

I returned to the barge feeling quite elated. I had joined the Resistance. I was now fighting for my King and country. I would become a hero and be presented with medals at Buckingham Palace after the war. Sweet dreams.

Lying in the bunk I could hear rifle shots in the distance. The French Resistance was at work. I hoped it was not Pierre and Pete. Sleep overtook me.

Another part of the Rance

Chapter Five

The next morning I woke up to find the sun shining into the cabin. It had been my first good sleep since leaving home to go fishing. In less than a week so much had happened; I had entered a scary new world. My life and my personality had changed forever.

I jumped into the canoe and went looking for clean drinking water. I found a very small stream that flowed into the reeds, the water tasted good and was clean so I filled my bottle and returned to the barge.

I had a swim off the barge and was ready for my French breakfast of biscuits and water. I found a good dry hiding spot, a cupboard at the back of the engine room where I could keep all my bedding and foodstuffs safely out of sight, but I knew it would not stand up to a thorough search of the boat.

I decided not to clean up the cabin, as this would just raise the suspicions of any intruder.

Deciding to use the canoe to explore the backwater, and keeping to one side and close to the reeds, I paddled to the junction with the main river. I pulled into the reeds where I could watch the traffic going up and down the river. I could just see the road bridge and part of the village that I had slipped past the night before, it was only about a mile away.

I was surprised how many barges were travelling up and down. Most had one Frenchman as helmsman and a deckhand. There were German soldiers on some of the barges, no doubt carrying supplies to and from St Malo. This would be a slow but very cheap and safe way of transporting less urgent things like building materials and heavy equipment.

Later, when I returned to the barge, I fished out the road map that I had taken from Pierre's kitchen. The railway bridges were at least eighteen miles from here by water and about sixteen if travelled overland. The trouble was I had to pass under the road bridge both ways and somehow get past the row of locks near Hédé. Either way, I would find it impossible to get back in one night if I was going to count the number of trains passing over the bridges after daylight. I thought a German soldier's uniform would be a great help. It would have to be from a little fellow to fit me. Where to find a small German soldier at night? Not in a bar, but maybe in a toilet outside a bar or perhaps just in a public toilet.

I decided to rest until dark and opened a tin of suspicious-looking meat: it was probably dog food, and finished the rather stale bread. You learnt not to be too fussy in the occupation. I dusted the table with Gerda's slacks to give them a much-used look. They fitted quite well; I slipped my precious bayonet inside them and wore my very grubby shirt on the outside. I then ruffled my hair and set off in the canoe.

It was now quite dark and I carefully concealed the canoe amongst the reeds close to the village; where I would be able, if necessary, to make a quick getaway.

I walked down the main street of the village keeping a good distance between myself and the few people still about. I arrived at the village centre, a large tree-lined Square surrounded by buildings, which included two cafés and a small hotel. Several army trucks were parked in the centre of the Square between two rows of trees. Near to the trees, there was the typical French circular toilet that exposed both your head and feet. Quite a lot of Germans were sitting at the tables outside the cafés. This must be a resting place for the truck drivers on their way to and from Renne. I found a spot a little way from the trucks and leant up against one of the trees. It was now quite dark. I stood there for some time watching the trucks come and go.

My problem as usual was how to dispose of the body. The discovery of a dead German in this situation would probably lead to the whole village being punished. The *Wermacht* showed no mercy in these cases.

Most of the trucks carried several soldiers in the back. They all jumped out, heading straight to the toilet and then drifted across to the cafés. After a time the number of trucks started to dwindle until only three trucks remained. Then a truck came in with just two men in the front and one in the back. He looked fairly short.

The three of them went straight to the café and sat down.

With no clear idea of what I intended to do, I quietly climbed into the back of this truck. There were several cases on the floor.

I undid the catches of one and felt inside with my hand. I had struck gold; the case contained hand grenades. I clipped two onto my belt and leant forward to get two more and at the same time I felt an arm around my neck. '*Que fait tu, Cherie?*'

I jerked around. 'Oh, my God.'

'*Zut.* You are English pig. I call my friends.'

I held my hand across her mouth as we fell across the case of grenades. I was on top of her and I pushed her head back, pulled out the bayonet with the other hand and brought it down across her throat.

It was all over very quickly and without a sound. I carefully undid the front buttons of her dress turned her over and slipped it off before it got too much blood on it. I felt around until I found her shoes and shoulder bag, grabbed two more grenades, wrapped them all in the dress and slipped out of the truck.

The Germans were still sitting outside the café. I crept slowly down behind the trees until I reached the far end of the square and crossing over to the buildings on the opposite side of the café, I quietly slipped down a side lane and was soon out of the village.

I had killed my first woman. It was so easy. I was getting quite good at the job, far less blood this time. It was not so much strength as technique.

In future I must train myself to think in French, I had given myself away too easily. The girl was a 'Jerry Bag'—a name given to female collaborators. Her death would be an example to the other girls in the village. A certain German soldier would now have a lot of explaining to do. He most certainly would have to die for this murder. Two for the price of one.

Back on board the barge, I placed the grenades at the foot

of my bunk, hoping I wouldn't kick them in the night! With the aid of the torch, I tried on the dress. It was quite a good fit. The shoes, slip-ons, were a bit tight but wearable. I suppose at sixteen I still had a bit of a girlie figure and my hair was now quite long. The shoulder bag contained lipstick and other cosmetics, a small mirror, a handful of Reich marks and an identity card. This could be even better than a German uniform. I would now be a 'Jerry Bag'. I took off the shoes and climbed into my bunk and was soon dead to the world.

Something cold was pressing on my nose. I slowly opened one eye to find a grenade resting against my face. I carefully slipped my hand under the pillow until I had hold of the bayonet. I sat up sharply swinging my feet to the ground, hitting my head on the top of the bunk.

'*Zut merd!*' My French was improving.

Pierre sat on the edge of the table, a big smile on his face. 'Not a bad reaction, Piglet! Try not to hit your head next time and I would suggest you throw the grenade away first.'

Standing up, Pierre shook my hand and pointed to a bag on the table 'I've brought your breakfast, fresh bread and a jar of confiture. So where is the girlfriend? I don't think much of her dress but then she won't be needing it now, will she, Piglet?'

I attacked the bread, spreading a large amount of strawberry jam on it, then slipped on my trousers and slipped out of the dress.

'I thought this could be a very useful disguise when I go to watch the bridges. The girl had a bit of an accident last night.'

Pierre laughed. 'I heard all about your visit to the village last night. I feel a little sorry for the poor soldier taking the blame for your bit of pleasure. Anyway I have news for you. I have other men taking care of the bridges so you will not be needed there now. However, we have something which will be much more fun for you.'

I finished eating the bread and washed it down with some water.

'As you might have noticed there is quite a lot of traffic on this canal and river system. At first the Germans were just using it for transporting small amounts of building materials and some farm produce. The situation is changing due to the Allied bombing of trains and the beginning of a fuel shortage. Most of their resources are now being directed to Russia.'

I noticed Pierre was now talking to me as an equal and not a teenager—I had graduated.

'We have noticed that the Germans are now using the French canal system to transport heavy equipment, large guns, ammunition, large quantities of cement and other building materials,' he continued.

'There is a canal and river system all the way from northern France to the ports like Brest, Lorient and St Nazaire where the Germans have their U-boat bases.'

I wondered where I was to fit in to all this and what sort of fun to expect.

'Due to an unfortunate accident of a friend and his nephew, I am now the proud owner of a barge and you, young Piglet, are my crew. He had only just bought this barge when they were both killed by the French Resistance for being too cooperative with the Germans. Their Identity cards have been altered slightly to suit you and me; your name is now Marçel and I am Pierre La Valle. We are to be picked up later today by another barge and will travel to Renne where our new home is waiting for us. The barge has been completely overhauled, it has been repainted, and has a new engine with all new fittings. We have an agent in Renne and will be able to accept our first cargo as soon as we take over the barge. We must dispose of everything here, so let's get started.'

We spread the sheet out in the canoe and piled the bedding and all my worldly goods onto the sheet, except for my bayonet, the torch and the compass, which I kept. We decided not to keep the girl's clothes and shoes or Gerda's slacks. We put the stones on top of the pile and I tied up my Christmas pudding.

As no one was about, we paddled to the centre of the river and heaved the large parcel over the side and because of its size, nearly followed it in. It was not safe to take the hand grenades with us so we concealed them by lifting a board under one of the bunks and carefully replacing it afterwards.

I was sorry to part with the canoe. We found a spot amongst the reeds where we filled it with water and some more stones. It sank out of sight; we would come and collect it at a later date.

We had a swim off the barge and lay on the deck in the sun. Pierre, unlike his boss Pete, was of medium height, quite thin with dark hair and a pencil-line moustache. He was a typical Frenchman. In his late twenties, I could see he was very fit and was looking forward to working with him.

Later that afternoon we finished all the food that was left, disposed of the rubbish and waded across to the riverbank.

'Marçel, when we get to the barge you will change into more suitable clothes and remember you are now a French boy. Because your language is limited, you will act like a retarded youth. Just nod your head and mumble a few words.'

We walked to the junction of the main river and sat and waited until dusk when the barge was due.

'By the time I have finished with you, Marçel, you will be able to speak fluent French.'

Top Level.
London. 1943

A secret cabinet meeting was held deep in a London bunker. Present—the Prime Minister, five senior Cabinet Ministers, Head of British Armed Services, Head of American Armed Services, Chief of British Intelligence MI5 and his American counterpart from the CIA.

'This, gentlemen, is a special one-off meeting, no record will be kept of this meeting and we have only one item to discuss. Except for two members present, all memories of the discussion and decisions made here must be erased from your minds. No one, I repeat no one must ever hear of our gathering and the decision made by us today.'

The Prime Minister continued, 'The war with Germany will eventually come to an end, there will be an enormous clean-up operation and many top Nazis will be killed or captured but gentlemen, there are thousands of evil men who will endeavour to escape our net. When final victory is achieved, the British public will be pleased to put the war years behind them and rebuild their lives. They will want to see a few top men tried and punished, but will not tolerate a witch-hunt where many more Germans would be killed.

'It is quite likely my government will be replaced by the Labor

Party and they will be more interested in the rebuilding of the country than wasting time hunting down the men responsible for all the atrocities committed during the war years. I therefore propose we set up a covert operation that will help certain high profile Germans to escape from their country. In the confidence of reaching a safe haven, they will fall into the pit that we shall dig for them and die quietly, unknown and forgotten.

'Gentlemen, the meeting is open for a short discussion. We all have many things to do.'

Fifteen minutes later a unanimous decision was made. The two heads of the secret services, MI5 and the CIA were given a free hand to jointly draw up a plan that would aid escaping Nazis and which would lead to their eventual elimination. The plan was to be put into operation as soon as possible and to continue for at least five years after the end of the war. The operation was to receive generous funding from the large amounts of money and treasures that would be recovered from the fleeing men.

'Thank you, gentlemen. This operation will now go ahead in the hands of the two organisations here tonight. No doubt there will be mistakes made but we will know nothing of this.' The Prime Minister gave the hint of a smile.

'Bear in mind that if any one of us here tonight were unable to forget this meeting and happened at some time to be indiscreet, their name would automatically be added to the list of escapees. Good night, gentlemen.'

Chapter Six

I t was dark when at last a barge appeared from the north. As it got closer, the engine stopped and it drifted slowly towards us. There was no one in sight except the man steering the barge. We swam out and quickly climbed the short rope ladder hanging over the side. The engine restarted and the barge picked up speed. We were on our way.

The man in the wheelhouse was bare-chested, with dark trousers and a peaked cap. After he had spoken a few words to Pierre, we made our way down into the cabin. We found a pile of grubby looking clothes on the table. Pierre slipped into some old navy blue trousers, a grey shirt, an old jacket with brass buttons and a peaked cap. I found a pair of heavy black trousers, an off-white T-shirt, an old windcheater and a peaked cap, without gold braid. We put all our old clothes in a weighted bag and threw them overboard. I was now Marçel with the nodding head, a fixed smile and an unintelligible mumble.

We passed under the road bridge and arrived at a stone jetty, where we tied up for the night. Later we sat around the table in the cabin drinking real coffee; black market no doubt, and eating large hunks of bread and cheese, with just a sharp knife for cutlery.

This was also my introduction to *Calvados*, a powerful alcohol made from distilled cider, Jean, our host, handed me a half-filled mug and insisted I finish it off. I took small sips at first and gradually got used to the strong cider taste and quite enjoyed the second mug, but soon after things started to spin around and I was unable to stand up.

The next morning, I woke up in one of the bunks with a splitting headache and feeling very sorry for myself. Pierre was at the table, dipping bread into a bowl of black coffee. I went on deck.

A lockkeeper's house

Later, Pierre joined me. 'We will shortly be passing through
the locks at Hédé; all our papers are in order. Here is an
identity card for you, the photo is a bit smudged but don't
worry it's near enough. Just watch me and Jean and do what
you can to help us when we go through the locks. Try not too
look like a novice and don't talk in English.'

We entered the first lock with another barge. When the
gates closed behind us, the water level in our lock rose up to the
level of the lock in front. There was quite a lot of turbulence as
the water poured in and we had to use poles to push ourselves
off the walls. I was standing in the bow when we passed under
the two railway bridges where I had killed Henry. I could not
resist making a rude sign to the guard standing on the bridge.
He pointed his gun at me, but he was smiling, I think.

'Don't push it, Marçel!' I could see Pierre was enjoying the
journey to Renne. His responsibilities would start once we
got to our own barge. 'We should arrive at the commercial
docks at about nine tomorrow morning, Marçel. I will go to
our agent's office, collect the keys and see if we have a cargo
waiting for us.'

'D'accord monsieur le capitaine.'

Pierre winced. 'Oh, God. Spoken like a true Englishman.'

We tied up near St Germain for the night, found a small bar
and tucked into bowls of *soup d'onion* with lots of *vin ordinaire*. I
was pretty exhausted by then, not yet used to working all those
lock gates. I was pleased when we passed out of the last of the
thirty-eight locks and arrived at Renne. We tied up at Renne's very
busy commercial wharf. A number of barges were being loaded
and unloaded, mostly by Frenchmen, and there were quite a few
Germans who appeared to be supervising the work.

Pierre went off to the office whilst I sat on the edge of the jetty. I was gazing at all the barges when I felt a tap on my shoulder. Two German 'Feldgendamerie' were standing over me, their silver plates that they wore on their chests shining in the sunlight. I stood up grinning and nodding my head. I mumbled some rubbish, hoping I was not overacting.

'Carte.'

I handed over my identity card. One of them gave me a push and I fell into the filthy canal water. When I climbed out, a small group had gathered around and were having a good laugh. With quite an effort, I maintained my silly grin. I was handed back my identity card and the Feldgendamerie moved on.

Pierre hurried over; more concerned than I, in case I lost my temper. 'Stay cool, Marçel you will get your chance one day. In the meantime, let's go and find our barge. Our barge is the fourth one out, at the end of this pontoon. We have our first job in the morning. We go back to Montreuil-sur-Ille where we will load sixty carboys of distilled water. We are to deliver them to La Roche-Bernard on the west coast. I think they will go on from there by road to St Nazaire where there is a U-boat base.'

We stepped across three barges, all manned, with some delicious smells coming up from their cabins, and arrived at our own freshly-painted barge. Pierre unlocked the wheelhouse door and we stepped inside what was to be home, for some time to come. Our barge was similar to the one we had just left, although a much newer version. The varnished wheelhouse was well equipped with a large steering wheel, brass engine controls, compass, a chart table, signalling lamp and various other bits of safety equipment.

The cabin was very smart. It had a gas cooker, a refrigerator and a good size wood burning stove. I opened the fridge door and looked into the cupboards, we had a fully equipped kitchen and someone had also made sure that we were well stocked with food and wine. At the far end, a small section had been panelled off and we had the luxury of a pump-out toilet, a shower and washbasin.

'Bring your torch, Marçel I have something interesting to show you.' We went down into the engine room. There was a large and powerful looking diesel engine, on one side of it a generator, complete with batteries, and on the other side, a good-sized electric powered bilge pump. The control panel was on the forward bulkhead, and alongside, attached to the bulkhead, rows of spanners and other tools. It all looked spotless; I intended to keep it that way.

At floor level, Pierre ducked under a small door. 'Follow me, Marçel.'

We crawled under the cabin floor and came to a higher section that was under the raised bridge. On either side were two tanks. The one on the right side was the fuel tank, and on the left side, a much newer tank had been placed on top of the old water tank.

Some oil drums were stacked in the gap between the tanks and the far bulkhead. Pierre moved some empty drums at the end of the old water tank and revealed a rusted panel.

'Slip inside this water tank, Marçel!'

I removed the panel and crawled inside the tank. I switched on my torch and was surprised to see that the inside had been painted white. On a slightly raised wooden floor there was a large mattress complete with pillows and blanket. Alongside there was a bucket and several large tins, one containing a torch, a mug, packets of biscuits and several bars of *Suchard* chocolate and in another tin there was a portable radio transmitter. A third tin contained handguns and grenades. A small tap in the ceiling with a length of hose ensured an ample supply of water. I noticed a small amount of light coming from the bottom edge of the tank. The inside of the tank was about eight foot long, six feet wide and four feet high. Once inside, the panel was clamped in place, and it could not be opened from outside. I backed out of the tank, closed the panel and replaced the empty oil drums.

'Our little secret, Marçel. If anyone happened to be inside the tank when a search was on, they would open the water tap and allow a small amount of water to seep out of the cracks in the side of the tank. This should convince the searchers that the tank is not a hiding place.'

Back in the engine room, Pierre explained the workings of all the equipment; I was shown how to start and stop the large diesel engine and to make sure the batteries were always fully charged.

'Our masters have equipped this barge especially for us, as you see it has a few hidden extras. Providing we are discreet and don't draw attention to ourselves, we have the potential to do a lot of damage to the Germans.'

Back in the cabin, Pierre had cooked potatoes and was frying up some steak, probably horsemeat but it smelt delicious. 'Boat people eat very well, they are able to trade with the farmers and the townsfolk and often get access to stolen German supplies.'

I opened a bottle of *vin rouge* and we tucked into our first good meal in a long time. I thanked my parents for introducing me to wines at an early age; this was one item we would not be short of.

'Marçel, I have to meet someone at a café near the docks. I will be some time, so just keep an eye on things until I get back.'

I washed the dishes and tidied up, determined to keep this cabin neat and clean. The bunks had clean linen, towels, pillows and blankets and the drawers under the bunks had an assortment of clothes to fit us both. I went onto the roof of the cabin and admired the star-filled sky. It concerned me a little that we were taking supplies for the German U-boats. This is not what I had planned to do—I just wanted to kill Germans.

When Pierre returned, I followed him back down into the cabin; he placed a large vet's syringe and a bottle of clear liquid on the table.

'A very small dilution of this liquid in the distilled water should, over a period of time, destroy the batteries of some of the U-boats. I'm putting this down into the old water tank until I get the opportunity to use it.'

Pierre returned from the engine room. 'Let's hope they don't send a German guard with us. In the morning, Marçel, we set off at dawn so get some sleep. We have a hard day in front of us tomorrow. I was soon asleep lying in the very comfortable bunk.

Part of the Vilaine River

'Wake up you land lubber we are moving out.'

I slipped on my clothes and climbed out on deck. It looked chaotic, the barges on our outside had already left, and the skipper on our inside was shouting at us to take in our ropes. Our engine roared into life and Pierre came up on deck.

'Prenez les cordes vite, Marçel.'

I pulled in the ropes and laid them out on the deck as I had seen Jean do the day before. Pierre put the engine into reverse and we slipped out of the line of barges. When we were well clear, Pierre gave the engine full speed ahead, the barge slowly swung around and we were heading down the canal. I went below and put on the coffee.

It was a glorious morning and Pierre let me take the wheel. It was not as easy as I thought—I kept overcorrecting and it took me some time before I was able to steer a straight course. We were heading north at about five miles per hour and had twenty miles and seventeen locks ahead of us, allowing for a lunch stop at Saint-Médard-sur-Ille we should arrive at Montreuil-sur-Ille at three pm.

Pierre decided to give me a French lesson. He started by teaching me the phrases we would be using when working the barge, although I already knew most of the swear words!

At midday, we stopped at Saint-Médard. We tied up to the jetty just behind another barge and Pierre went off to telephone our time of arrival at Montreuil. He returned with loaves of fresh bread and a dish of *Pate de Campagne*. We washed this down with red wine and after a short siesta, leisurely cast off and headed for Montreuil-sur-Ille.

There were four trucks waiting at the jetty when we arrived. We tied up and Pierre started up the winch that pulled back the hold cover. This was done by a series of cables attached to the winch and saved us a lot of manual work. The trucks backed up to the barge and a group of soldiers passed the carboys of distilled water into the hold. Down in the hold, Pierre showed me how to place them close together, so that they would not fall over and break. When they were all in place, we ran a rope through the front row of the frames of the carboys, and then attached the ropes to the sides of the hold.

Pierre closed up the hold cover. Back in the wheelhouse, a German NCO was waiting for Pierre to sign the paperwork.

'My name is Klaus. I shall travel with you to make sure you do not steal from the *Führer*, I'm sure you will make me very comfortable on this voyage.'

Pierre gave a grunt of disapproval. 'I will show you a berth as soon as we finish the paperwork.'

There were sixty carboys written in on the consignment note: we had taken seventy onboard. 'We have ten more carboys on board than you have put down on the paperwork, why is this?' Pierre demanded.

'A poor soldier's perks! Don't worry; I will pay you for the extra transport cost.'

Pierre grabbed the German by his shoulders. 'I will carry your perks on one condition only, soldier. You will give me five hundred Reich marks for the transport cost and you will also give me a signed receipt for this transaction.'

Klaus gave Pierre a sly smile. 'Why not, you would never have the nerve to use the receipt. My word as a German will always stand up against yours, Captain.'

Klaus gave Pierre the five hundred Reich marks and Pierre wrote out an account to Klaus for the delivery of the extra ten carboys. Klaus was not pleased when I added my name to the delivery note, and would have been even less pleased if he had realised that he had just signed his own death warrant.

Although it was a little late to set off that evening, Klaus insisted that we start on our way. It was dark when we tied up at Saint-Medard-sur-Ille and Klaus went off to the local café. We stayed onboard and cooked a light meal.

'You realise Klaus has created a situation where we are now able to dispose of him once he delivers his ten carboys to his accomplices. We now have his signed note, which I can give to the *Feldgendamerie*. They will believe him to be a thief and deserter.'

I chuckled. 'I will be delighted to play my part when the time is right Pierre. In fact I might even sharpen my bayonet in anticipation!'

It had been a long day; we were both tired so we turned in. Sometime later, I heard Klaus scraping along the deck. He sounded drunk. He came down the steps, threw himself on his bunk and started snoring like the pig he was.

We set off at dawn the next morning, another bright sunny day. I was finding it hard not to talk in English, so I kept well away from Klaus and Pierre. I felt sure I had convinced Klaus that I was quite mad and perfectly harmless.

We reached Renne about nine am; Pierre decided not to stop as we had plenty of fuel onboard to get to our destination. I went below to make some sandwiches; Klaus followed me down. I was standing at the table cutting bread when Klaus moved up behind me; he pressed himself against my back and his hands came around and he started to feel my private parts.

'Does that feel nice, dumb boy?'

I realised sixteen-year-old boys are just as much at risk of being molested as girls. I quickly moved to the fridge to get some ham for the sandwiches. I gave Klaus my innocent smile, finished making our lunch and moved quickly up on deck. Klaus followed close behind me, I gave Pierre a quick sign. He guessed something was going on and knew that Klaus was in for a very nasty shock.

Klaus shared our lunch and had his fill of wine—I was thinking of the condemned man and his last meal.

'You will stop at Messac. I will discharge my ten carboys there.' Klaus looked at the map on the chart table. 'We should be there late this afternoon. That is good.'

We were travelling at a steady six miles per-hour, which was a reasonable speed on the Villane River and we arrived at Messac at six pm. Klaus disappeared and returned some time later with a truck and three men.

Pierre opened the hold so that Klaus and the three men could load the truck. There was no one about when they finished and the truck drove off with the carboys and the three men.

'We go.' Klaus ordered. He was looking very pleased with himself and we were happy to get going so quickly. We ca off and continued on our way.

Klaus went down into the cabin. Pierre turned to 'Marçel I think it would be a good time now for you and do your job. Are you quite sure you want to?'

I could feel my heart beating faster with excitement, anticipation. 'Just try and stop me, Pierre.' He gave m look, just for a moment I felt superior; I knew he was r of doing what I was about to do. To me Klaus was ju slaughtered and I went eagerly down the steps to t'

Klaus was sitting at the table counting m brushed passed him and moved over to my be

and felt for my bayonet, which I kept under my pi̇ỉ.
was right behind me.

I smelt his foul breath; he was breathing heavily as
his arms around me. I allowed my rage to take control, I sv
around but Klaus stepped back and I was only able to gr.
his neck. He ran back to the table, picked up the bread kni̇
and came straight for me. I moved away from the bunk—we
stared at each other for a few seconds then Klaus lunged at me
with the knife. I stepped back, Klaus launched himself at me,
as he came forward, I ducked and Klaus was off balance—he
had taken a step too far. I stood up inside his arm that held
the knife, slipped one arm around Klaus's waist and with the
other, slit his throat. Klaus literally died in my arms.

Pierre appeared from the wheelhouse. 'Marçel, did you have
to make such a mess?' He went back to the steering wheel.

I lifted Klaus onto a large sack and cleaned up most of the
blood. I was a little puzzled as to why I always felt so elated
after a killing. Maybe the rape had made me a little unbalanced.
Klaus had made sexual advances to me but that was not always
the reason why I killed. I joined Pierre in the wheelhouse.

'As soon as it's dark enough, we will get him on deck, lash
him carefully to that crowbar next to the winch and then
dispose of him.' Pierre was laughing. 'We really must get some
heavy weights and a few large sacks on board if you are going
to make a habit of killing our passengers, Marçel.'

Pierre allowed the barge to slow down until we were just drifting. Between us we dragged Klaus up to the wheelhouse. I took
the wheel and brought the barge back on course whilst Pierre
carefully lashed Klaus to the heavy crowbar.

It was now getting dark and we were going through an area

with woodland on both sides of the river. We moved to the centre of the river and stopped the engine. There was no one in sight so we carefully rolled Klaus over the side. He sank immediately. Pierre crossed himself; we started the engine and were on our way.

I spent the next two hours scrubbing and cleaning the cabin; every trace of Klaus was removed. It was not easy finding our way in the dark but we finally arrived at Redon.

The Redon commercial area was much larger than at Renne. Redon was the junction for several canals and rivers. We found a vacant berth at one of the jetties. Pierre decided he would report to the *Feldgendamerie* first thing in the morning. We both found it hard to sleep that night.

Early next morning Pierre had nipped ashore and returned with an armful of freshly baked *baguettes*; I don't know how he managed to get hold of this fresh bread when everything was in such short supply.

Pierre set off to the *Feldgendamerie* to report the missing Klaus. He used all his skills as a lawyer to explain how Klaus had forced us to carry his stolen cargo and to deliver it to his friends at Messac. He had then gone off with his friends in their truck and we presumed he had deserted the army. Pierre stated that he felt it his duty to report Klaus to the *Feldgendamerie* as Klaus was both a thief and a deserter, and whatever his nationality, he should be punished. Pierre also produced the signed delivery note as proof that Klaus had stolen the ten carboys from the *Wermacht*, and that we had done everything possible to help the *Feldgendamerie*.

Pierre had done such a good job that the Germans actually thanked him for all his help. They came back with him to check our cargo, and all our papers and identity cards. We were told we had to stay where we were until they had spoken to their counterparts in Renne. Later in the afternoon, they returned to tell us we could continue on our way. The Renne *Feldgendamerie* had been watching Klaus for some time and had hoped to catch him stealing army supplies. They thanked us again for our help.

We decided to make it a complete rest day and to leave for La Roche-Bernard early the next morning, so we spent the rest of the day topping up the fuel tank, washing the decks and generally tidying up the cabin and wheelhouse.

Pierre went below to prepare a special meal in honour of our departed guest Klaus.

I stayed on deck.

Passing Messac on the Vilaine

Chapter Seven

A very smart barge with several Germans on board was approaching us. As it brought its stern close in to us, I noticed a very attractive young girl standing on the deck, waiting to throw the ropes across.

'*Prenez les cordes gaçon.*'

I slipped the loop over a bollard and we both ran to our barge bows.

'*Alors, prenez.*'

As I caught her rope she gave it a sharp tug; caught off balance, I fell straight into the river. When I surfaced I could hear shrieks of laughter coming from the newly arrived barge but I don't think the Germans appreciated the joke. The girl dangled the rope over the side and I swam over and pulled myself on board. By then Pierre was on deck and took the rope from the girl and made fast.

I was very wet and quite speechless at seeing such a pretty girl. She had long black hair, with a gypsy look about her, and a lovely smiling face. This was a girl of my dreams.

'*Je suis navrée, m'sieur. Je m'appelle Simone, et vous?*'

I put on my best French accent, '*Je vous en prie Simone. Je m'appelle Marçel.*' I certainly had no problem accepting her apology.

One of the Germans waved to me to get off their barge. I noticed through a partly open hatch they were carrying torpedoes, which would account for the Germans on board.

'*Plus tard, Marçel.*' Neither had I a problem with that.

Pierre and I tucked into grilled trout washed down with a great wine from Saumur on the Loire River. As soon as we finished clearing up, I went on deck in the hope of seeing Simone. A few minutes later there was a thump as she jumped onto our deck.

'*Venez avec moi, Marçel.*'

I followed her onto the jetty and we both ran up the main street until we came to a park. The moon was out, and for a while I became a boy again. We found some swings and pushed each other so hard that the swings began to rock dangerously. We ran wild around the park, unleashing all the pent-up energy we had stored up from living in the confines of our barges. At last totally exhausted, we returned slowly to the jetty. Simone had talked a lot, I understood very little of what was said and I replied when I could, but mainly with just the odd grunt here and there.

Back on board, we stood together on the stern deck, both staring at the bright full moon and the star-filled sky. The only sounds on this magic summer night were the frogs calling to each other, and the occasional splash of a fish jumping out of the water.

Simone touched my hand lightly. It was like a small electric shock that made my fingers tingle. I took her hand in mine and wanted to say something, but again I was lost for words.

'I think you are English boy, Marçel! Don't worry; I will not give you away. I am a true French girl and will do anything to save my country.'

I was not surprised. 'You are quite right, Simone, but that seems a long time ago. The *Gestapo* are looking for me; but I have found safety here on the barges and I think I shall be able to help, in a very small way, in the liberation of your lovely France, from the evil Germans.'

'You are one of us, Marçel, and I know we will always protect each other. My father and I do what we can and sometimes we are able to pass back useful information to the Resistance.'

I turned towards Simone and she moved closer to me. I looked down at those lovely shining eyes, I was mesmerised by her beautiful oval shaped face, her little turned up nose and lips that I so badly wanted to kiss. Simone leant forward and her lips gently touched mine, I was overcome with warmth, joy and excitement. I took her face in my two hands and kissed her lips with just the lightest of contact. I felt myself shaking. I was floating on air. Suddenly our kisses became stronger and wilder and then just as suddenly we both pulled back, so as not to break the magic of our new bond.

The kiss had sealed our two hearts together and we both knew that we were in love and that nothing could ever change that. We laughed and cried together, hugged and then we parted. Simone returned to her barge and I went slowly down the cabin steps and collapsed onto my bunk. I had never felt so much joy in all my life.

I woke up the next morning to the sound of our engine running. Pierre was casting off by the time I got on deck. I could see Simone's barge moving away in the distance.

Anti-aircraft guns were firing and were leaving puffs of black smoke in the sky. Several aircraft passed very low overhead and then a terrible explosion.

To my horror, a flash of fire erupted from Simone's barge. The barge lifted and then disappeared into an enormous cloud of black smoke. When the smoke eventually cleared, there was nothing left but a few bits of debris floating on the water.

I stood in the silence that followed, completely stunned. On this fine summer's day, my world had been blown apart.

I started to cry. I fell on to my knees, weeping, howling like a dog and shaking all over—I wept for all the things that had happened to me in the past few days. I don't know how long I cried. At last I felt a hand on my shoulder.

'So you really are human after all, Marçel. You know of course Simone would have known nothing; it all happened so fast. Maybe better she died that way than perhaps killed sometime later at the hands of the *Gestapo*.'

I slowly got to my feet, completely emptied of all feeling. Was this a punishment for all the terrible things I had been doing in the last few days?

Pierre put his arm around my shoulder. 'Come, Piglet, we have much to do.' He restarted the engine. 'Take the wheel, Marçel, we must continue on to La Roche-Bernard. Study the map, the river is much wider from now on and it gets quite tricky in places.' I could see Pierre was also very upset.

'You know, Marçel, Simone's father was one of us, he had informed the Resistance that a large consignment of arms was due to be sent through by this route to St Nazaire; he could not have known it was to be on his barge, and that he would die for passing on this information.'

'Pierre, how could the RAF have possibly known which barge to attack?' I was crying again.

'Come on, Marçel, this is where you prove that you are a man. This is a very dirty business we are in. A member of the Resistance must have managed to paint a large sign on the roof of the wheelhouse at some stage. They would have radioed London last night to say the barge with the sign on the roof was leaving Redon at first light.'

I couldn't believe what I was hearing. 'We are going past now, Marçel, keep well to the far side of the river and just keep looking ahead.'

The banks on both sides of the river were badly scorched, I found myself staring at the water although I knew there could be no remains left after such an enormous explosion.

Oh, Simone, why couldn't I have been with you?

We passed over her grave and continued down the river. It was some time before I finally stopped sobbing.

I have never cried much since.

The river was quite tricky at this point. I had to take care to keep within the marker buoys. I very nearly took the wrong turn, which would have taken us to Nantes and the River Loire. Because the river was flowing strongly at this point, I had to keep the barge at full speed in order to maintain steering control.

Pierre appeared with some enormous sandwiches and a bottle of wine. He took over the wheel and I tucked into the meal. I had a deep feeling of sadness and the wine helped to dull the pain.

The memory of Simone has always remained with me. I have not met anyone like her since.

Nor would I ever want to . . .

Chapter Eight

Ashmore Manor

Peter Lonsdale passed through the front door of Ashmore Manor shortly after lunch. It was a warm summer's afternoon in 1943. Pete was old at twenty three, slightly built, just over six feet tall and very fit. He had a mop of fair hair, a well-shaped face and a sunny disposition.

An only child with a strict father and a doting mother, Pete's father would beat him for the slightest misdemeanour when he was just a child. His mother, being helpless to intervene, would often retire weeping to her room. Pete's father died of a heart attack when he was fifteen years old and life for Pete and his mother from then on changed for the better. Mr Lonsdale senior had left his wife and Pete quite well-off financially. So when he finished school at seventeen, they spent the next two years touring France and Germany where Pete became fluent in both languages.

When war started, Pete volunteered for the army and because of his fluency in French and German, he was posted to a special service section that operated from this manor house in Somerset.

In November 1940, Pete went to visit his mother in London to find his house had just been destroyed and his mother killed in an air raid. He watched as the fierce fire continued to destroy all the houses in his street. This was to change Pete forever. That night he declared his own war on Germany.

His red Triumph sports car looked a little out of place amongst all the camouflaged army trucks and jeeps parked on the gravel drive. Pete was also the only person wearing civilian clothes.

Having identified himself at the reception desk, Pete was escorted to a waiting room where he sat for a short while before being invited into the plush office of the Head of Operations.

'So you made it back safely, Pete.' The person addressing Pete was also in 'civvies'. Stephen Harvey had spent many years in the diplomatic service and refused to wear a uniform. Because he was dealing with senior officers of the three Services, Stephen had been given the rank of Air Vice Marshal, a rank he preferred not to use.

'You have done excellent work in northern France helping to organise Resistance groups, and your barge on the canals has already started to show us some good results.' Stephen invited Pete to sit down and then offered him a cigar, which Pete refused.

'It's progressing well. We have some very good men in the

field now, but as the Germans become more organised, we are bound to have heavy losses in the next twelve months. Stephen, I expect you know all about my sixteen-year-old boy from the Channel Islands.'

'Indeed I do. I think you should handle that boy very carefully. He seems to have psychopathic tendencies, which is useful to us at present but could prove a problem to you at a later date. Pete, you have been summoned here today because of a very unusual request that I have received from our lords and masters. We have been requested to set up an organisation, with absolutely no links to any of the existing Government or service departments.'

Stephen continued, 'I believe you are the best person to set up this 'business venture'. Although you will not have any help from us to organise and run this venture, you will have the blessing of both the British and American Governments and perhaps at times a certain amount of protection. We want it operating as soon as the Germans realise the war is coming to an end, which should be sometime next year and we also expect your business venture to continue for at least four years after the war has ended.'

Pete was intrigued. 'This sounds interesting, Stephen, but what sort of business. And who pays all the bills?'

'You stand to make a large amount of money in the next few years, Pete. We want you to set up an underground line of escape for minor Nazi war criminals. They will come to you in Germany, in the belief that you will deliver them through France and Spain to Portugal, where a waiting ship will convey them to South America. We will supply the ship, and you will man it. Their journey will end somewhere in the Atlantic.'

Stephen sat back, a wicked smile on his face. 'None of this

evil scum will be able to warn their colleagues of this 'journey to the death'. They will be changing their identity and will be expecting to start a new life in South America so no one will ever know of their fate. We owe this 'payback' to the thousands of Jews who we believe are being transported to the death camps in Germany. Every day thousands of men, women and children are dying in the gas chambers and at present we are unable to help them. As to costs and your payment, dear boy—these scum of the earth will be loaded with gold and precious artefacts, stolen from the Jews. As you are running a private business, we will turn a blind eye to the stolen gold, but we would expect, at some time in the future, the artefacts to mysteriously arrive at the British Museum, where they might eventually be returned to the surviving Jews.'

La Roche Bernard

Pete was intrigued with the idea and realised the enormous financial gain to be had from such a plan. 'So is this to be my retirement pension?'

Stephen was smiling again. 'As a matter of fact, yes. I would suggest you bring your 'Piglet' back here for some intensive training. He could make a very useful partner for you, especially in disposing of any difficult customers on the way. When you are ready to start this enterprise, you will both return to France. At a suitable time you will both have to be officially eliminated by us. I think you might be burnt to death in a barge somewhere. I'm sure the French Resistance would cooperate in this matter, especially if they knew you were transporting guns and ammunition to St Nazaire for the Germans. All we need is just a couple of charred bodies!'

'I like the whole idea, Stephen. Two of us would certainly be enough to carry out this scheme. We will set up a series of safe stopovers all the way to Portugal. There we can operate our ship from a quiet part of the coast.'

'We will have another agent who will find and direct clients to you. How you organise yourself is entirely up to you, Pete. We just want to know that the Nazis trying to escape the net are being quietly eliminated. We have decided to write off the barge—it will be your property from now on. You will no doubt be able to use it as a base. If you can get a cargo of ammunition, then blow the bloody thing up.'

They stood up and shook hands.

'I must say I like the young 'Piglet', Stephen. He has guts and with some of your intensive training, he and I will make a good team. I also appreciate that 'Piglet' and I could become very rich in the process!'

'If you stay alive that long, Pete. No one will realise quite what you are doing. You will be in danger from all sides. I understand you return to France tonight. Good luck. We are bringing back two RAF boys on your plane. When you rejoin the barge, you will drop Pierre off at Pontivy. He is needed by the group that are operating near Brest.'

Pete drove down to the village pub, his thoughts on the serious implications of the meeting. It meant going underground for the next six years or even longer. It also meant the killing would go on long after the war was over. What sort of life could one lead after so much slaughter? Would he and 'Piglet' be able to retain their hatred of Germans for all that time?

Pete entered the pub.

He had time for a couple of pints and a game of darts.

Chapter Nine

I took over whilst Pierre went down below, reappearing with the syringe and the bottle of clear liquid. 'I'm going down into the hold, Marçel, so keep a good lookout and call me if you have a problem.' Pierre eased back the throttle until we were travelling at half speed, then disappeared into the hold.

Sometime later he joined me in the wheelhouse holding the empty bottle. 'I managed, with great difficulty, to inject a small amount of this special liquid through the corks of ten random carboys. Over a period of time, when this distilled water is used to top up the battery systems in the U-boats, the batteries will become contaminated and if the U-boats are at sea, they will become disabled. This liquid is undetectable in the carboys and there is no trace of damage to the corks where I used the syringe.'

One hour later, Pierre took the barge up a small side river called the Trevelo. When we were well out of sight, we pulled in to the bank. I went below and fetched the radio transmitter and Pierre went off with it into the surrounding woodland. I didn't question him when he came back later, but I knew he had gone to send and receive messages to England. I guessed they would only be interested in the success of the air raid and the contaminated distilled water, but not in the death of Simone and her father.

We returned to the main river and continued on our way, arriving at our destination La Roche-Bernard, quite a small port that was crawling with German sailors. There were several patrol boats anchored near the small jetty. Our cargo was quickly discharged and loaded onto trucks where it would go on by road to St Nazaire.

The paperwork completed, we were told to move out as several barges were waiting to unload. As there were no locks to negotiate on this trip, we set off and headed straight back to Redon.

It was dark when we arrived. Pierre had sent me down to the cabin to prepare our evening meal so that I would not see the place where the barge had been destroyed that morning.

We tucked into an enormous meal of stewed lamb and potatoes and lots of red wine. We both got very drunk and I only vaguely remember Pierre helping me into my bunk.

The next morning, I woke up with a splitting headache. Pierre had just returned from our agent and was making coffee. 'We are to take a large consignment of produce containers to Pontivy. This is a rich farming area. On the way, Marçel, we have a very interesting job to do for our masters. We head north up the Oust River, to a point where the River Aff joins the Oust. There we pick up two passengers and take them to a remote place near the Lanouee Forest. We then meet up with another French Resistance group. They specialise in organising landing strips and the handling of 'Airdrops', our two guests will be picked up by an aeroplane and flown back to England.'

We moved the barge farther up the jetty until we were opposite a very large stack of assorted crates and boxes. Pierre opened up the hold, and a group of men came over and started to load the hold with the crates, boxes and tubs. When the hold was full, the men carried on stacking the crates on the deck, until Pierre had to stop them from completely blocking out our forward vision from the wheelhouse.

'We should do very well out of this cargo, Marçel.' Pierre was smiling. 'We are dealing with French farmers and will barely cover our fuel costs on this run, but we should make it up on the way back with a load of their produce.'

We set off late that afternoon after refuelling and topping up the water tank. One of Pierre's black market friends had delivered a large crate of supplies earlier that afternoon. It was starting to rain. I cast off the bow rope and because of the deck cargo, had to run down the jetty to get to the stern end of the barge.

This time we headed northwest and on the River Oust, part of the Brest-St Nazaire canal. I was glad not to be passing the place where Simone had died—I now had even more reason to want to kill Germans. We travelled quite slowly up this lovely part of the country, as Pierre wanted to arrive at our meeting place at dusk. The rain had stopped and the sun was out so I had a sleep on the cabin roof until I heard the engine slow down.

Pierre took the barge up the small side river, and then carefully turned around so that we were pointing the way we had come.

'If anyone was watching they would think we had made the wrong turn. Just keep your eyes on both sides of the river, Marçel, and tell me if you see any signs of life.'

I could tell Pierre was a little nervous; he was holding our signalling lamp and staring into the reeds on the riverbanks. 'Our guests will signal to us with a mirror or a torch. We must be absolutely sure that no one else is in sight before signalling them to come out to us.'

At last, just as it was getting dark, we saw a slight flash of light coming from the reeds. Having made sure no one else was around, Pierre signalled them to come out. A small rowing boat emerged from the reeds and two scruffy men in very dirty RAF uniforms climbed onto the deck. The third man immediately turned the little boat around, rowed back and disappeared into the reeds.

'Marçel, take our guests straight down to the cabin.' He turned to the two men. 'You must stay down below out of sight until I tell you to come up. You must only come on deck when either Marçel or I tell you.'

I took the men below and Pierre started the engine. He headed down to the junction of the rivers and then turned the barge until we were once again heading up the main river.

The two airmen, Geoff and Anthony, had been shot down in northern France during a daylight raid two weeks earlier. Their *Beau* fighter-bomber had been hit by anti-aircraft fire but they had both been able to parachute safely to the ground. They had hidden in a forest until they were found by an old couple, who took them to their cottage. The old people were in contact with the local Resistance and each night they had been passed on from one safe house to another until finally they were delivered to us.

Pierre called down, 'Marçel, show these gentlemen their sleeping quarters and make sure they know how to access the water.'

I took them through the engine room to where the storage tanks were, and showed them how to open the cover leading into the old water tank.

They crawled into the tank and I was just able to follow them in; it was a very tight squeeze. There was ample room on the mattress for both of them and I showed them how to get water by using the tap above their heads. I also showed them how to allow water to flood the floor of the tank, and thus allow a little water to seep out of the cracks in the old tank. This would indicate to anyone searching that the water tank was quite unusable. I could see they were not impressed with their sleeping arrangements but too bad, they would be very safe there if the barge were searched. I warned them not to talk or make any sound, if the Germans came aboard to search the vessel.

I had survived so far by keeping my wits about me and I was not going to let anyone place our 'ideal set-up' at risk. I decided I was even prepared to kill our own people if they were at any time to endanger our enterprise. Pierre and I had created, with the use of our barge, great potential for doing a lot of damage to the Germans—with the radio, we were in an ideal situation for passing valuable information on to the Allies.

Back in the cabin Pierre put his head down the hatch. 'Marçel, come and take over for a while. We will tie up to the bank before dark.'

Up in the wheelhouse, I had to concentrate on the steering as the light was fading. A hand came up holding a mug of red wine but I was not in a celebratory mood. In fact, I was consumed with sadness and anger. I had no wish to talk to the two airmen; one of their planes could easily have killed Simone.

We found a suitable place where we were able to tie up and made fast to some convenient trees. It looked very quiet with no houses in sight. Sociable Pierre was well away and he and our guests were soon into their second bottle of Merlot. I cooked some eggs with slices of ham and tomatoes. After we finished our meal I cleared up.

'Pierre, I think you chaps should keep the sound down.' I poured myself a mug of wine and went and sat quietly on deck. It was another still summer's night, the sky was clear and filled with millions of stars. It was like the sky two nights before, only this time I was alone.

Pierre came noisily up the steps. 'What are you doing up there, Marçel; come and join the party it's not often we have guests.' I was looking at the riverbank. It must have been a bird that moved, but it was enough to make me very aware of our situation.

'Pierre, I have never been a party person, anyway I think we should keep a watch whilst we have these airmen on board.'

Pierre grunted. 'I also think our guests are making far too much noise; sound travels a long way over the water especially on a night like this.'

Geoff and Anthony came up on deck. I was starting to get

angry, this was too much. 'I think you two chaps should stay below especially when we are travelling in daylight tomorrow morning. I also think we should each do a four-hour watch on deck tonight, starting from now. Only one person should be on deck at a time.'

Pierre was looking at me; I could tell he was impressed. 'Marçel is quite right. Geoff, you take the next four hours then Anthony will relieve you. Marçel and I will then take over. If you hear or see anything, wake Marçel and I and then you must both go quickly down to the water tank. As for tomorrow, you will have to stay below in the cabin. If it becomes necessary, you will have to go down into the tank.'

We left Geoff on deck and went below, I checked to make sure there was nothing to show that more than two people occupied the cabin and shortly after, we turned in. Still on edge, I decided not to undress. I was worried that Geoff and Anthony were on different wavelengths to us. Our life was all about survival, kill or be killed, we were always on the alert, never sure when we might be arrested and killed by the *Gestapo*.

I was just drifting off when I heard the sound of engines. I flew up the steps. 'Quickly! Get down below, Geoff.' As I followed him down, a German patrol boat flashed its searchlight directly on to the barge. I grabbed an empty bottle of wine and scrambled back on deck. The patrol boat slowed down and stopped just a few yards from us.

'*Attention. Qu'est-ce qu'ily a?*'

I lurched forward and replied in my best drunken French, '*C'est le capitaine m'sieur. Il est soul encore.*'

I felt a tug at my trousers. 'I'm certainly not drunk now,'

whispered Pierre. The patrol boat's engine restarted and to our relief continued up the river.

Pierre and I were up at first light. As it would take at least ten hours to reach our destination (it was only about twenty miles, but we had to pass through twenty or more locks), we decided to take it slowly.

We needed to meet our contacts at dusk as there was some distance for our two airmen to travel to the arranged landing strip. I was to go with them to the aircraft in case anything went wrong with the pick-up and I would be forced to bring the two men back to the barge. Pierre would stay on the barge and be ready to move off if things got out of control.

Geoff and Anthony were sound asleep. I wished they would stay that way all day. We decided to give our guests a special treat—when they finally came to, we gave them *ersatz* coffee and some rather stale German rye bread for their breakfast. I hoped they would appreciate our occupation fare.

We travelled slowly up the river, the sky was overcast and it was raining quite heavily. Most of the locks were between the attractive towns of Malestroit and Josselin. The castle at Josselin is quite imposing. Geoff and Anthony stayed in the old water tank. A pack of cards and a bottle of wine kept our guests occupied, whilst Pierre gave me a French lesson in the wheelhouse.

Once past Josselin, as there was very little traffic on this part of the river, we were able to tie up to a deserted jetty and have a very late lunch. This time we made up for the skimpy breakfast and gave our guests fairly fresh French bread, ham, *saucisson* and an assortment of cheeses.

The castle at Josselin

Just after seven pm, we turned off the main river and into the entrance of the Lie River. We pulled into the bank and were partly concealed by tall reeds and overhanging branches. I looped the ropes around two tree trunks so that we would be able to make a quick getaway if necessary.

The light was starting to fade; the rain had stopped and the clouds had lifted. It would be ideal for night flying. The small village of Les Forges was in the distance and beyond it a large dark area, the Forest de Lanouee.

After a while, we saw a man standing on the bank. He signalled to us to come over. I went below and told Geoff and Anthony that we were ready to go and to follow me. I told them to move as quietly as possible and not to talk. I had the compass and small torch in my pocket and slipped the bayonet into my belt. We dropped into the water and waded ashore. Our guide signalled us to follow him. When we reached the top of the bank, I took a compass bearing on the opposite riverbank, where we had entered this part of the river. This would guide me back to where the barge was tied up.

We climbed up through rough scrub until we came to a road at the top of the bank. Our guide paused to make sure there were no Germans on the road, we slipped quietly across and were soon moving through the forest on level ground. I noted that we were still more or less on the same compass bearing; this would make it easy for the return journey.

About thirty minutes later, we came to a large clearing in the forest. We were led to the remains of a building—just four walls and no roof. The floor was covered with tall weeds and rubbish. We sat up against one of the walls and waited.

With my limited French, I managed to talk quietly to our nameless guide. We were at a derelict World War I training aerodrome that the Germans had not yet put to use. His Resistance group had cleared a short landing strip, which they had then disguised by placing rubbish, tree branches and oil drums on the landing area. When an Allied aircraft was due to land, they cleared the strip and then replaced the rubbish after the plane left.

He told me the aeroplane tonight would stop very close to where we were. I was to tell Geoff and Anthony to run out as soon as they saw it starting to turn around. They had to move very fast as the plane would not stop for more than a few seconds. I explained this to them and I knew they would not waste a second in dashing across to the aeroplane. In the distance we could hear the sound of heavy bombing. We could see a large red glow to the northwest. This would give the cover and protection needed for our light aircraft.

It would be here soon. After picking up the two men, it would join up with other aircraft and would receive protection for the return journey to England. It did not occur to me that I could have joined the two airmen and escaped to England.

We heard the approach of a small aircraft. Our guide disappeared.

Standing near the entrance of our building, I saw two figures running down the landing strip placing a row of torches as they ran. As they got to the end of the strip, I saw the aeroplane coming in to land. The plane was coming straight towards us. It slowed down and started to turn. Geoff and Anthony ran off towards it and I wished them good luck.

They reached the aeroplane before it had completed its turn. I think it was a 'Lysander' Aircraft. A figure jumped out and I saw our two airmen get in. Suddenly I heard the gunshots, the Lysander lifted off, started to climb and then hit the ground in a ball of fire. In the glaring light I saw two Resistance men run along the landing strip and collapse to the ground. The figure that had left the Lysander was coming straight towards me. Just before he reached me, a German soldier appeared from nowhere and leapt on him. They were both on the ground.

I reacted instantly; I sprang forward and launched myself at the dark figures. Holding my bayonet in both hands, I landed on top of them and my bayonet went right through the German's throat and into the ground. My face was covered in blood; German blood.

The body underneath wriggled out from under the German. 'Not bad at all, Piglet.' I recognised the voice.

We ran into the forest. I could still hear gunshots behind

us. The French boys were keeping the Germans occupied. I hoped they would have the opportunity to slip away as well. As soon as we were sure we were not being followed, we stopped to catch our breath. Pete put his arms around me and we gave each other a powerful hug.

Pete gripped my shoulder speaking quietly, 'Am I pleased to see you, Piglet. Looks like I might owe you one.' I was very pleased to see Pete again. I felt a strong bond had now been established between us.

We moved on silently through the woods until we reached the road. An army truck was parked a little way farther up the road. We had been very unlucky; a passing truckload of German soldiers had seen the small aircraft coming in. They arrived at the landing strip just as the aircraft was taking off and a lucky shot must have hit the fuel tank. We heard later that they had been pinned down by the Resistance and had all been killed. Three Frenchmen also died that night.

We moved father down the road, I followed Pete as he wriggled to the opposite side. Later I would be trained to do this properly and not graze my hands and knees as I did that night. When we were safely across the road, I took a compass bearing. We headed to the right for about one hundred yards, I took another bearing and we were then on course to the barge. We slipped down the bank and arrived at the spot where I had left it.

No barge.

'I think Pierre might have moved back onto the main river when he heard the gunshots, Pete. If we walk to the mouth of the river we might just spot him.'

We got to the bend and waded through the reeds until we

could see up and down the main river. Pete spotted the barge on the far bank about two hundred yards downstream.

'Race you across, Pete! I need to wash the German blood off my face and you smell of deodorant! You're not in London now!'

I sat on the opposite bank waiting for Pete. Pierre had the engine running by the time we clambered aboard and we moved off slowly heading up the river.

After drying out, I took over the steering wheel, whilst Pete and Pierre went below to discuss the events of the evening. With the engine running slowly, we crept up the river until we were well past the branch of the river where we had landed earlier that evening. After another two miles, we reached a place where we were able to bring the barge into a small side turning, out of sight of the main river. We tied up to the grass bank, again, with the help of two convenient trees.

We were all feeling a bit subdued by now. The loss of the aircraft, the pilot and the two English airmen we had tried to help. Also, we did not know how many Frenchmen had died in the fighting.

'So just when I was beginning to enjoy life on the canals, I have now been ordered to move up to Brest; You don't have to worry, Marçel, Pete knows the canals far better than I. He has just as many contacts as I have, so you certainly won't starve.'

Pete got up and gave Pierre a friendly slap on the back. 'Pierre, you know, with your talents you really are wasted here on the barge. Anyway you will meet lots of girls when you get to Brest and you will be able catch up with some of your old friends.'

Pete continued. 'I'll leave the barge early in the morning

and will rejoin you when you get to Pontivy, the day after tomorrow; that's when I officially take over the barge. In the meantime, I'm going to get some sleep in the water tank, just in case we have visitors in the night.'

Pete disappeared into the engine room and Pierre and I turned in. I lay in my bunk thinking of the two RAF men. I had been the last person to speak to them; I had wished them 'Good Luck'.

Chapter Ten

We set off at daybreak. Pete had slipped ashore before it grew light and was now on his way to meet us at Pontivy. We only had twenty-four miles to travel but we had a staggering sixty-four locks to pass through on the way, so we expected to reach Pontivy about lunchtime the following day.

The journey to Pontivy was uneventful, apart from working our way through the locks and in places, finding the river quite narrow. We spent that night in one of the locks. The next morning we eventually came to a road and a railway bridge and finally arrived at Pontivy.

A group of Germans were standing on the jetty. They jumped aboard and immediately started to search our barge. The patrol boat that had stopped to look at us three nights before was tied up at the end of the jetty. Pierre, guessing what was happening, went down into the engine room to turn off the engine, he reappeared wiping grease from his hands.

The officer, the captain of the patrol boat, approached Pierre. 'Why has it taken you so long to get to Pontivy? What have you been doing all this time?'

Pierre showed the officer his greasy hands. 'Water in the fuel lines, *Herr Capitaine*. The fuel today is of such poor quality! I spent hours cleaning the filters and fuel lines.'

The search not having revealed anything, the German Captain ordered his men off the barge. As he was about to leave he turned to Pierre. 'Did you hear any gunfire the night before last?'

Pierre replied eagerly, 'But yes, *Herr Capitaine*. We guessed you Germans were out hunting in the forest. There are plenty of deer in the forest.'

Shortly after, the patrol boat and the Germans set off down the river. Pierre gave them a friendly wave as they passed. The *Capitaine* returned a frosty salute.

The local farmers arrived and started unloading and sorting the crates and boxes. After we finished our lunch, Pierre decided not to wait for Pete as he thought we might be getting another visit from the Germans, this time from the *Gestapo* regarding our presence near the shooting two nights ago.

'They won't bother with you, Marçel, as long as you act the dumb boy. If Pete gets back when they are here, he can easily explain that he has just arrived to take over the barge.' Pierre packed a few things in a bag, warmly shook my hand and left. I was sorry to see him go, and did not wish him good luck.

The hold was almost empty by now so I went down and started to sweep it out. The crates had left quite a mess and our next cargo was to be farm produce. I found an old dustbin and carried all the rubbish and dumped it at the rubbish area, which was just behind the jetty.

I was about to return when a car pulled up at the jetty and four Germans in civvies, *Gestapo* men, jumped out and headed straight for the barge. I dropped down behind the pile of rubbish and backed away until I was able to hide behind some bushes. Dumb boy or not I was not going to take the chance of being recognised as the 'Piglet'.

I could see one of the *Gestapo* men talking to the last of the farmers, who was tying up his load of crates. The farmer pointed in my direction. I was going to have to bluff my way out of this, so I slid back to the rubbish heap, picked up the old dustbin and started walking back to the barge. I forced myself to grin, tried very hard to whistle, but very little sound came out.

As I stepped on to the barge, I was grabbed by the collar and forced down into the cabin. One man had stayed on deck. Two held onto me, and the other who was in charge, hit me hard across the face. I was trying to keep my silly grin, and started to nod my head. For this I received two more blows to the head. My nose started to bleed.

'*Ou est le capitaine gaçon?*' he demanded.

'*Le capitaine il est parti m'sieur. Le nouveau capitaine arrive bientôt.*'

I received one more blow for luck, then they let go of me and I slipped to the floor half stunned.

The four *Gestapo* men were on the jetty when Pete arrived, carrying an old kit bag on his back. After lots of shouting and arm waving the *Gestapo* men got in their car and drove away.

I was standing by the table trying to stop my nosebleed when Pete came down into the cabin. 'Looks like you came off worst this time, Marçel. Never mind, you are now my 'First Mate' and from now on 'Mate', you and I are going to create absolute havoc amongst the Germans.' Pete threw his kit bag at me, I caught it and nearly collapsed with the weight. 'Have a look in there, my boy; I'm glad you didn't drop it.'

The bag was filled with detonators and explosives, two revolvers and two Sten guns (light machine guns) with a quantity of ammunition. 'I must say,' Pete was grinning, 'I was a little concerned when I saw your friends on the jetty. However a little friendly chatter and all is now well.' Pete produced a flask from his pocket. 'Lets celebrate our new start and afterwards you can cook me my first meal, God help me!'

'Pierre thought it prudent to set off early and so avoid meeting the *Gestapo*. A wise move as it turned out,' I said as I passed some papers to Pete. 'He told me to make sure you looked at all the paperwork, and to check all our permits. We will be getting a load of farm produce in the morning which we are to take back to Renne.'

'That sounds good, Marçel. We will have to make a fast run to Renne as it will be perishable cargo. I need to see some contacts in Renne anyway. By the way, I thought we might blow up the railway bridge, which is farther down the river. We could do it on our way back to Renne.'

The next morning at daylight the farmers started to arrive with their produce—a mixture of cauliflowers, cabbages, carrots, potatoes and other vegetables. An agent for the farmers was writing out consignment notes. I was given the job of double-checking the number of packages for each consignment.

They arrived mostly by horse and cart and just a few came with their tractors and trailers. The farmers organised the loading and I must say the produce was all carefully stacked in the hold, with gaps to allow air circulation.

Pete had gone into the village to see his friends and reappeared just when I was checking the last load of cauliflowers. By the time we finished the paperwork, the farmers had all disappeared into the village bar. It was after twelve pm so we decided to get going straight away. I worked the winch and closed up the hold, careful to leave a gap for air circulation.

Twenty locks after we left Pontivy we saw the railway bridge in front of us. I took the wheel and Pete carefully studied the underside of the bridge. There was a guard standing at each end and we could see that the guardhouse was on the opposite side of the river.

The locks were all hand operated so I had to help the 'Eclusier' (lock keeper) each time to open and close the gates. Because the locks were so close together, by running ahead and opening the next lock we were able pass through a lock in less than ten minutes.

It was dusk when we passed the village of Gueltas and shortly after we found a secluded inlet. Pete made some coffee and produced some large pieces of *gateaux* he had brought back from the village. Pete went down to the 'water tank' and returned with a bag of explosives and detonators. 'My friends have supplied us with transport. We can be at the bridge and back here before dawn. There will be no connection between us and the sabotage to the bridge as we should be well down the river by then. I will use a timing device which will enable us to be well clear when the bridge blows.'

We set off along the riverside track at two am. A few minutes later, we saw the remains of an old barge on the riverbank. Pete disappeared into some bushes and returned wheeling two bicycles.

Keeping to the riverside we soon slipped passed Gueltas and followed the dirt road. We arrived at the main road and the river bridge, quite close to the railway bridge, our target.

We concealed our bikes in some bushes, carefully crossed the road and slipped down to the riverbank moving cautiously along the bank until we arrived at a sharp bend in the river.

Once around the bend we had a good clear view of the bridge and could see the red glow of a cigarette coming from where the guard was standing right at the end of the bridge. I wondered how many guards had been killed just by having a lighted cigarette in the mouth—such an easy target.

We waited patiently for at least forty minutes when at last we heard the slow approach of a train. As it got close to the bridge, Pete moved forward and climbed the bank until he was just under the bridge. I crept up behind Pete until I was close to where the guard was standing. The guard was watching the train.

As the train came by us, the guard stepped back and I stepped forward. My bayonet gained itself another notch. I quickly pulled the dead guard off the bridge and joined Pete.

'Pass up the explosives, Marçel.' Then followed the longest ten minutes of my life as Pete finished his task and set the time clock. We had a thirty-minute start before the bridge blew. We hoped the guard at the other end would not decide to walk across the bridge to see his mate.

We crept back along the bank and up to the road, crossed over, retrieved our bicycles and rode like mad down the dirt track. We had just passed Gueltas when we heard a rumble and saw an orange glow behind us. We kept going and soon arrived at the place where we had picked up the bicycles. We hid them in the bushes and ran back to the barge.

Pete started the engine and I pulled in the ropes. It was five am with just enough light to see our way. As soon as we were able, we ran the engine at full speed. We were now far away from the bridge and would not to be connected to the sabotage.

Our breakfast of coffee, bread and cheese never tasted so good; Pete and I were still riding high. 'You really have become an expert killer, Marçel, I would not like to be your enemy!' I leaned across and gripped Pete's hand. 'Don't worry, Pete, you are quite safe with me . . . at present.' Our high spirits were soon to become overtaken by tiredness. It had been a long and busy twenty-four hours.

Chapter Eleven

We kept the engine running at full speed most of the next day, except for when we passed through the locks. We wanted to get the farm produce to its destination as quickly as possible, especially as it was such warm weather.

It was almost dark when we tied up at Redon. We went ashore and found a café still open and had a good meal of river perch and *pommes frites*, washed down with a carafe of *vin du pays blanc*.

We made an early start the next morning and were due to arrive at Renne in the afternoon. Before leaving, Pete had telephoned the office at Renne and given our expected arrival time.

Pete insisted we speak only in French and I soon found I

was starting to think in French. I was quite enjoying myself and took every opportunity to talk to people as we passed through the locks or tied up at a jetty.

'Have you thought about your future, Marçel?'

I was standing next to Pete in the wheelhouse whilst he negotiated our way past two extra large barges. 'I could never go back to my family now Pete. I've moved into a completely different world and I have so much blood on my hands. I have to make my own life now; it might not be so easy for me to stop killing people.'

I thought about it for a few moments. 'After the war Pete, I think I would like to stay here and become a *Batelier*, and have my own barge. At least I wouldn't have to pass any exams to qualify!'

'It is quite possible, Marçel, that you could be employed in some undercover work which could last for a few years and continue well after the end of the war. It might not mean living on the barges, but you could be travelling on canals in different parts of France; you might even make a lot of money. Would this interest you?'

'Tell me more, Pete. Would I be working for you?' I certainly was interested—I might even be able to kill a few more Germans.

'If you were to take this path, Marçel, you would be working with me, not for me. We would be running our own business in Europe with the doubtful blessing of Her Majesty's Government.'

I took over the steering from Pete; this was getting very interesting. 'Just think very carefully about what I am proposing before you make any decision, Marçel. If you decide to join me in this enterprise, you will have to fly back to England fairly soon. In England you will go through some very special and intensive training. This will be extremely hard for you; but I've no doubt you will survive the course and you will certainly become very fit and will learn the essential principals of self preservation and of course improve your killing skills!'

I had not seen Pete in such a serious mood. He seemed to be making a difficult decision himself.

'Once you return to France, Marçel, until the work we are undertaking is finished, the only 'let out' for you is your demise; we will be involved in something far more dangerous than anything you have done so far. You will see, and take part in, the killing of a lot of very evil men and women. You will be meeting people who have been involved in the death of thousands of innocent men, women and children. So just think very carefully before you come to a decision.'

Pete strode off to the bow, he just stood there for a while and I could sense his deep-felt anger. I knew that Pete was referring to certain things that were happening in Germany and I also knew Pete would show no mercy to the people involved in the running of the death camps. We had heard rumours of the mass killing of the Jews in Europe, but we still had no idea of the full horror that was to be revealed to the world in 1945.

I did realise that once I became involved in this 'business venture', I would be unable to retract, as with my knowledge of the plans to punish these people, I could endanger the lives of those still involved; they would probably have to kill me. Pete and I had the same mentality, if killing was justified, then we could both kill in cold blood and feel no remorse, almost a feeling of satisfaction, if not pleasure. I knew we could work well together. I liked the idea that we would be involved with the people trying to escape their punishment at the end of the War. Even better, we would be paid for it.

The agent and several men were waiting at the jetty when we arrived at Renne. As soon as we tied up, the agent took all the paperwork and set up a makeshift desk on the jetty. I opened up the hold and the gang of men started to unload the produce. Pete and I did our best to separate all the consignments. It was a complete waste of time; the wholesale merchant mixed everything up again when he came to load up his trucks.

When the last of the cargo had gone, we swept up the rubbish in the hold, moved the barge across to a pontoon and joined a row of empty barges.

'I might be away for a few days, Marçel. If I am more than a week, go across to our agent's office. Joseph will tell you what to do. In the meantime have a rest, work on your French and keep out of trouble.'

Pete went ashore to see the agent. Afterwards he went off to meet his 'friends'. I tidied up the deck and had a sleep on the roof of the cabin.

The next four days seemed endless. I spent a lot of the time studying the French books that Pierre had given me. I talked a little to one or two of the *Bateliers* on the barges nearby, but I still had to be very careful with my accent. One woman tried speaking to me in English. I gave her a blank look. It worked.

I found some paint and went around the deck touching up any small patches of rust I could find. We had plenty of food on board so I had no reason to go ashore.

Occasionally a barge would move off to pick up a cargo and another empty barge would arrive to take its place. Life on the barges in summer was good. There were whole families on some of the barges; they seemed to be generally quite a happy bunch of people.

I had plenty of time to seriously consider Pete's offer to join him in his future plans; I liked the idea. I had started a new life and was enjoying the excitement. The boy had become a strong, ruthless and determined man. I would continue this life for the next few years and I hoped to make a lot of money. If I turned this proposal down now, Pete might have to eliminate me as I already knew too much of his plans. Maybe one day I might even have to eliminate Pete.

A very scruffy looking Pete returned on the third evening. Much to my relief, he looked very pleased with himself. I grilled the large piece of steak that he had brought with him and over the second bottle of *vin rouge* he told me just a little of what he had been doing.

'I have been in contact with the French Resistance boys who take care of the secret landing strips. They lost three men the night I came in and killed all the Germans that attacked us that night. They took the bodies and the truck to another location, well away from there and blew up the truck. They made sure all the German bodies were destroyed in the fire.'

I refilled Pete's glass and he continued, 'They went back to the landing strip to clean up, removed the remains of the *Lysander*, buried the three English men in the forest and covered up the remains of the fire with debris and old bits of burnt timber. The Resistance boys are convinced the Germans still have no idea of the existence of our landing strip. They are keeping a man close by, to see if anyone comes by there in the next two weeks. After that they believe we can use the landing strip again. In the meantime, Marçel, we have a cargo of fertilizer to take to Redon, and then on to Pontivy, which means another return cargo of farm produce.'

Lockkeeper's house on the Oust River

'I shall be pleased to get moving again Pete. By the way, I accept your offer of a partnership in the human 'dust cart' business. I am prepared to go all the way with you in eliminating the scum.'

'Pleased to here that, dear boy. I was going to eliminate you if you had said no but I was pretty sure that would be your answer, Marçel, so I took the liberty of organising your return to England and a six month training course for you when you get there. I shall join you much later in England.

We are expecting the invasion of France next year and I still have much to do over here.'

It took a third bottle of wine before we were both ready to turn in. We drank to our future partnership. We both knew our friendship would be strong enough to see us through the times ahead.

The next morning we moved over to the jetty. We were loaded with an assortment of fertilizers, which were to be delivered to Redon and Pontivy. This time the barge was low in the water, weighed down with its heavy cargo. We would have to be careful not to become stuck in shallow water.

It was midday before we left Renne. We kept up a steady speed down the Villane River but it was almost dark when we arrived at Redon. I did not go ashore this time.

An agent with his gang of unloaders appeared soon after daylight. Whilst they were unloading part of the cargo, Pete went ashore and returned with fresh food, wine and several freshly baked *baguettes*.

'Marçel, we will be receiving another guest tonight; a surprise for you, someone you have seen before.'

I was puzzled, I had met so few people and they were mostly Germans. 'I hope this is not going to be another air disaster Pete. I'm already trying to face up to flying across to England.'

We set off again later that morning and headed up the Oust River to Pontivy. It was another fine summer's day. We had to pass through all the locks again, which made the journey interesting, but hard work.

Late afternoon, we passed the small town of Malestroit. Further up the river we pulled in to an old jetty and tied up for the night. The town was quite deserted. There were several derelict cottages and a tumbled down barn that must have been abandoned a long time ago.

After a light meal and lots of freshly made coffee, Pete went below to the old water tank and returned with the two Sten guns. 'I can't let you practice firing this gun, Marçel, but I can at least show you how to hold it and fire it. I'll also show you how to strip it down and reassemble it.' After several attempts, I was able to strip and reassemble the gun and felt quite confident that I would be able to use it, if necessary.

It was now close to midnight. 'Time for us to head off to the pickup point. It won't be landing this time, Marçel. Our guest will, with luck, be landing by parachute. There should be just sufficient light to spot the white parachute.'

I slipped my good friend, the bayonet, in my belt, put the torch and compass in my pockets and joined Pete on the deck. The two Sten guns had shoulder straps, which left our hands free to climb up and over the old jetty.

We followed a dirt track that ran past the cottages and directly away from the river. I took a compass bearing of the barge. This amused Pete, but I was not taking any chances in case I had to return to the barge alone. The track was overgrown as it had not been used for a long time. We eventually came out of the trees and passed through some rough scrubland, which gradually turned to grassland. I could smell cattle and heard the lowering of a cow not too far away. In the distance ahead, we could see another line of trees.

There was just enough light from the new moon to show up the track to the pilot of the aircraft. We stood and waited.

'I will need your torch, Marçel; I just hope we are alone here tonight.'

It seemed ages before we heard the sound of aeroplane engines. There were a large number of them and they were flying very high up. 'On their way to bomb St Nazaire tonight, Marçel.'

Another aircraft was approaching. It was flying much lower and it had a much quieter engine. As it got nearer, Pete pointed the torch in its direction and signalled VE in Morse code. The aircraft flew overhead and disappeared, following the other aircraft. About ten minutes later, we heard it coming back towards us. Pete repeated the signal. The plane passed overhead and continued on its way.

We were both searching the sky. 'There it is, Marçel, about two hundred yards ahead.' We started to run towards the white patch. Halfway there, Pete grabbed me. We stopped, stood still and listened. Except for the distant rumbling, all was quiet. We ran up to the figure rolling up the parachute and bent down to help. '*Bon soir mes enfants,*' said a woman's voice.

'Welcome back, Gerda. We will talk later but now we must get back to the barge as quickly as possible.' Pete took hold of the parachute and we quickly made our way back to the cottages. Pete gave me the parachute whilst he went ahead to make sure it was safe to return to the barge. Once on board, we cast off and continued up the river with the engine running as quietly as possible. It was just becoming light.

Our first job was to pack the parachute in a strong bag. (Pierre had laughingly brought some large bran bags that he called 'body bags' when last in Redon. 'These are especially for your use Marçel.' He had joked.) We placed some heavy weights in the bag and then dropped it over the side, making sure we were in the centre of the canal.

By the time we reached the first lock it was daylight; we had to wait for the *Eclusier* to open the lock.

I was in the cabin making coffee when Gerda joined me. 'So, Marçel, you are the famous boy who witnessed my brother's death.' Gerda's French was far better than her English was. 'Klaus was a good man and I loved him very much. He was so unlucky to have a sister on the opposite side. I do not blame you, Marçel; the *Gestapo* were on to Klaus long before you arrived on the scene. I'm glad he died as he did, and not at the hands of the *Gestapo.*' Gerda moved across to me and kissed me lightly on the forehead. 'So, we are friends now, Marçel?'

I stood there recovering from the kiss. Gerda was a tall, slim and very attractive blonde, I guessed in her early twenties. I had not noticed this on our first encounter. She looked very fit and had small, lovely breasts. I was starting to blush. 'Why yes sure. I think you're lovely. I mean yes, yes let's be friends.' To add to my confusion Gerda started to undress. She removed her flying overalls and stood in front of me, in her pants and bra. Gerda was laughing at me as she slipped on some old clothes, let her hair down and put on a pair of worn shoes.

I was smitten. *Lucky Pierre.* I had to turn my back on Gerda for a few minutes. 'The little boy is shy, yes? You will have to get used to living with an old woman for the next few days.'

Pete came down the steps; Gerda put her arm around me. 'I think I embarrassed the boy, Pete. We are good friends now—he is lovely.'

We sat around the table enjoying our coffee. Gerda explained her reason for being with us. 'I am to go to Paris to work there until the invasion of France which hopefully is next year. I am to help prepare lists of war criminals who will be dealt with by the Allies, both in France and in Germany. As soon as the Allies start moving into Germany, I am to follow them and work with British Intelligence in Germany. Pete, when the time comes I will be able to furnish you with a separate, detailed list of minor criminals. My condition for taking on this job was that I could spend a few days here with Pierre before going on to Paris.'

Gerda took Pete's hand. 'I was told you could arrange that for me, Pete. By the way, for my cover I am your wife having a short break on the barge. I have the necessary papers for that.'

Pete had a wicked smile on his face. 'That, Gerda, is your bunk over there, and the one on the other side is only, and I mean *only*, for me.'

'You flatter yourself, Pete; I would much rather share with Marçel—I like them young!'

The *Eclusier* was shouting and the lock gates were opening. We started the engine and moved into the lock waiting for the water to rise before the other gates could open. Apparently, the Germans had not spotted the parachute descending the night before.

By eight that evening we had reached Gueltas, having had an uneventful trip. We ate lunch on the deck, taking advantage of the warm sun and enjoying the superb countryside. I found it difficult to take my eyes off Gerda, who kept us laughing all the way. After having a hilarious and slightly drunken evening tied up in one of the many locks, we retired for the night, making a late start the next morning for the rest of the journey to Pontivy.

We tied up to the jetty at Pontivy and the agent came aboard. Over a bottle of *vin rouge*, Pete introduced his wife Gerda. The agent told us he would unload the fertilizers the next day and arrange to load the produce for Renne the day after.

Pete went off with the agent to meet his contacts in the town. Gerda went off to get eggs for the evening meal. I set about tidying up the cabin.

Gerda was soon back but it was quite late when Pete returned. Gerda cooked us a beautiful omelette with lots of French fries and a well dressed salad.

'I have made contact with the group from Brest. We have set up a meeting for tomorrow night. Pierre will be coming back with us, so we need to take an extra bicycle. Our bicycle friend is going to borrow the extra bikes for us.' Pete was looking thoughtful. 'Maybe you should stay here, Gerda. I don't have a good feeling about this meeting.'

'Just you try and stop me, Pete. Anyway you need me; I'm very good with a gun.'

Pete gave Gerda a thoughtful stare. 'It may very well come to that. Tomorrow night we will travel for about ten miles along a dirt road and through a forest until we come to Lake Guerledan. There is a deserted cottage on the edge of the lake.'

The next day the farmers arrived to unload and collect their fertilizers for the following season. When they finished, we had the task of cleaning out the hold as the smell of the fertilizers would contaminate the fresh produce. In the end we washed down the sides and then had to pump out the water.

We ate very little that evening; I think Pete and I were

thinking of our disaster at the airstrip. I also worried about taking Gerda with us. We decided to leave at ten pm so that we could arrive at the meeting point at midnight.

We found the bicycles at the back of the rubbish dump and set off down the dirt road heading north. Pete and Gerda each had a Sten gun slung over their shoulders and I had one of the revolvers and my trusty bayonet, tucked in my belt. As usual, I had my torch and compass. We took it in turn to hold the spare bicycle; this slowed us down a little. The track ran into the forest just past a crossroad.

'We'll leave the bikes here and walk the rest of the way, chaps.' I could see by now Pete was very alert and ready for anything. We concealed the bicycles in the bushes.

'I want you to spread out. I will lead, Gerda, follow about ten paces behind me, and you, Marçel, keep well behind to cover our rear. If you see Germans coming up behind us, it means we have walked into a trap. Fire your revolver to warn us and get the hell out of here. Make a large circle back to the bicycles and wait.'

We moved slowly and silently amongst the tall trees until the old cottage came in sight. Pete had stopped dead; he was staring at what looked like a decorated Christmas tree. Gerda ran up to him 'Oh no—my God! It can't be.' She ran forward.

'Come back, Gerda.' Pete tried to grab her it was too late.

Four French Resistance boys were hanging from the tree. One of them was Pierre.

Gerda screamed and all hell broke loose.

Germans ran out of the cottage firing their guns as they ran towards Gerda. She stood still firing her Sten gun, sweeping her fire back and forth. Gerda fell to the ground. Pete moved forward, firing as he went. He took Gerda's arm and dragged her back to the bushes.

I fired my revolver at the Germans, then ran ten yards to the left and fired again. I fired and ran again. It was enough to distract the firing from Pete; to give him time to lift Gerda onto his shoulders and dash deep into the forest.

The Germans were heading in my direction. I decided discretion was the better part of valour and retreated up the track. As soon as I thought I was far enough away, I turned sharply to the right and into the forest. I started to make a large circle that I knew would take me back to the bicycles.

I heard someone coming up behind me and slipped behind a tree trunk. It was Pete, carrying Gerda. Some sort of instinct made me hold back. I let them pass and waited behind the tree. I heard a rustle of dead leaves by my tree. I stepped out. The look of surprise, which quickly turned to horror on the German's face as I slit his throat, gave me some satisfaction after seeing Pierre hanging from the tree. Perfect timing, I thought, as the German crumpled to the ground.

I could still hear gunshots. I quickly caught up with Pete and Gerda, who had partly regained consciousness. She had been hit in her arm and her leg and was in shock. We reached the bicycles—four bicycles and two riders.

We managed to get Gerda wedged onto the crossbar of Pete's bike, with her top half draped across the handlebars. 'You keep going, Pete. I'm going to try and hide these bicycles so that our Pontivy friends can retrieve them later.'

Pete gave me Gerda's Sten gun; I gave him a push start and he was away. 'I'll catch up with you later.' After a very shaky start, Pete managed to control the bike sufficiently and set off to Pontivy.

I wondered why I could still hear shots coming from the cottage. I guessed I had not seen the last of the Germans. I found a suitable spot deep inside some bushes where I concealed the two bicycles. It was the best I could do but would not stand up to a thorough search. I hopped on the remaining bike and rode as fast as I could to catch up with the others.

I was about halfway to Pontivy when I heard the motorcycle coming behind me. I knew what to do. I left the bicycle at the side of the road and stood behind a tree, close to the road. The motorcycle and side car came bumping down the road, it slowed down when the two Germans saw the bicycle and before it stopped, I stepped out and fired the Sten gun until it ran out of bullets. After checking that they were both dead, I rode like hell until I reached Pontivy and left the bicycle by the rubbish heap. I saw a figure come over to collect it.

There was no sign of life on the barge. I made some coffee and waited in the wheelhouse. A little later two men appeared, pushing a wheelbarrow. Pete and the other man gently lifted Gerda on to the barge and brought her through the wheelhouse and down into the cabin. Pete thanked the man who then set off back to the village pushing the wheelbarrow. 'Gerda has been very lucky, Marçel, She has two bad flesh wounds but no serious damage. I'm afraid, Gerda, we will have to hide you in the old tank. With those wounds you will be a dead giveaway when the Germans come to search us.'

We managed to get Gerda down below. I got into the tank first and carefully pulled her in and onto the mattress. The local midwife had managed to dress Gerda's wounds and had given her some sort of homemade knockout drug.

Pete poked his head in to the tank. 'I think you should stay with Gerda until she becomes fully conscious, Marçel. Gerda is going to need someone to calm her when she comes to and remembers exactly what happened.'

I was more than happy to stay with Gerda. I guessed she would need someone to talk to—waking up in the tank would be very scary.

'That's fine by me, Pete, as long as you bring down some hot coffee.' I covered Gerda with the blanket, arranged her pillow, sat by her and gently stroked her head. I felt so sorry for Gerda; she had lost both her brother and her husband in such a short time.

Sometime later I realised she was awake. She was lying very still, tears running down her face. She began to sob, first quietly and then her whole body started shaking, I held her tightly. Our faces were touching and my tears joined hers. I had nothing to say to comfort her.

After a while, Gerda stopped sobbing but still clung to me. We stayed like that for a long time. Finally, she released herself, took my head with both hands and gave me a long but gentle kiss on the lips. 'Thank you, Marçel. You don't realise how much you have helped by holding me and sharing my grief.'

Sitting up, she pulled back her hair, brushed herself down and gave me a big smile. 'So now we both have a mission. One day I will avenge Pierre's death and help to kill many of the vermin that are living amongst my people. You will come and visit me in Paris, Marçel. We will share a real bed next time.'

I slipped out of the tank and joined Pete on deck. It was just starting to get light. 'Gerda will be alright now, Pete. She's had a good cry and is ready to carry on.' Pete raised his eyebrows and gave me a knowing smile. 'Pete, she just needed a shoulder to cry on.' I was not amused.

'We had better be ready. We will be searched any time now. Take everything of Gerda's down to the tank, Marçel.'

I cleared Gerda's bunk and took down all her gear, with a mug of coffee and some sandwiches.

At first light a very agitated agent appeared. 'All hell has broken loose in the district, Pete. We are expecting the Germans to search the town any moment. Luckily the local Resistance followed you to your rendezvous last night. They saw what had happened at the cottage and when the firing started, they attacked the Germans from the other side of the cottage and gradually withdrew to the west. The Germans followed, believing it was an attack by the same group from the northwest. Later some of our other men found the motorcycle that they dumped into the river. They cleaned up the scene of the killing and disposed of the two dead Germans.' The agent paused for breath.

'Where is the woman, Pete?' Pete was smiling, he appeared to be quite unruffled by the situation. 'Don't worry my friend. Once again your boys have done an excellent job. 'The woman' is well hidden. The Germans will never find her. Our worry is that we have an informer somewhere in our midst. We must find him and kill him.'

'I have a good idea who he is, Pete. One of our farmers had a grudge against Pierre from a court case before the war. Tonight he will die slowly—and very painfully. Now we must start loading your barge. The farmers are arriving. We know nothing of any shooting last night.'

We were all busy loading the farm produce when the

Germans arrived. We were immediately forced to stop work and were all lined up on the jetty whilst the barge was carefully searched.

The farmers and workers chatted and laughed amongst themselves. I realised this was all part of the cover; the French were experts at fooling the Germans, especially when they had something to hide. I noticed Pete was having a friendly chat to an officer standing on the jetty.

Every inch of the barge was carefully searched, but the water tank remained undiscovered. At last, the Germans clambered off the barge, looked underneath the jetty and searched all around the area.

There was a lot of shouting and door banging coming from the town. A house-to-house search was in progress—no Resistance men would be at home and certainly no weapons would be left in any of the houses.

Finally, the Officer in Charge waved to the farmers to carry on loading. The Germans climbed into their trucks and headed off to join the soldiers searching the town.

'We were very lucky this time, Marçel. That officer told me that a good part of the produce goes to the German forces; because of that they have been ordered to go easy on this town and the local farmers. In other places a lot of good, innocent people would have been shot today.'

We kept on loading until the last of the produce was stacked in the hold. It was quite possible the Germans would return and carry out another search. When all the paperwork was completed, I slipped down to see how Gerda was. She said she had slept most of the time but was a bit worried when a German started tapping on the tank. They missed the well-disguised panel at the end of the tank.

The Agent shook our hands and wished us well; he was pleased to see the back of us this time. He untied the ropes and we started the engine and with great relief we pulled away from the jetty. I got the winch working, pulled the cover over the hold and took over the steering from Pete. He went below and helped Gerda out of the tank and up to the cabin. I could soon smell coffee. It was midday and we had not eaten since yesterday.

'This will keep you alive until tonight.' Pete passed me up a mug of coffee and a hunk of bread and sausage. 'Keep a careful lookout all around in case that patrol boat appears. If you spot any Germans at the lock gates we will have to quickly get Gerda back into the tank.'

We passed under the bridge that we had tried to destroy on our last trip to Pontivy. A number of workmen were busy repairing the damage and unfortunately, it would soon be back in use. At least it would have been out of action for a while. 'I should have climbed out to the centre of the bridge. The damage would have been far greater and it would have been much more difficult to repair.'

Pete went down to the cabin. All these minor damages of the railway system by the Resistance kept the Germans on their toes and tied up a very large number of their fighting men.

We were kept busy opening and closing the endless number of locks. Pete was fending off whilst I helped the *Eclusier* but there was no sign of Germans at any of the locks. At dusk we pulled into a quiet part of the river and tied up for the night.

In contrast to our lively evening on the way to Pontivy, we had a very quiet and sombre meal of pork chops and fresh vegetables, supplied by the farmers. Gerda was feeling much better physically and decided to go back to the safety of the tank for the night. This meant we could all have a good night's sleep.

The next morning it was raining when we set off. We decided to leave Gerda in the tank as Pete was going to make contact with 'his friends in Rohan'. At Rohan, we tied up to the jetty and Pete disappeared into the village, returning an hour later laden with supplies, including some fresh bread.

I had the engine running and we immediately cast off. Much later, we passed the small side river, which was near the landing strip. I wondered when I would be flying to England; it could be from this same landing strip.

Pete brought Gerda up to the cabin. It had been arranged that Gerda would be met at a point north of Redon. She would have to take the slow route, being passed down a line of safe homes until she eventually reached Paris. Gerda would have to avoid Renne, where she was well known. She would go southeast past Angers, Orleans and Fontainebleau and then on to Paris.

Gerda's wounds, although painful, did not restrict her movements and she was now able to walk. It would take a long time for her to get over the shock of seeing Pierre hanging from the tree. Pierre's death had cast a deep shadow over the three of us. These events just strengthened our determination to do everything possible to help destroy the enemy.

I spent most of the day at the wheel whilst Pete stayed with Gerda. In the late afternoon, we passed the old castle at Josselin and tied up for the night at Roc-Saint-Andre; it was to be the last meal we would have together for some time. We drank a lot of wine that night, especially Gerda who shakily stood up to make a slurred thank-you speech.

'I will never forget how you helped me get through those first few hours, Marçel. Pierre and I were devoted to each other—life will never be the same again—but with so much fear and hate around us; it will not be too difficult to move on. There is so much to do. We have to end this terrible war, punish those responsible and try to re-rebuild Europe. You, Pete and I will do our small parts but I know that what we will be doing will play an important part in the future.'

Gerda took my hand. 'Some time in the future, you come to Paris to stay with me. By then, Paris will be free and maybe you make love to me; that I would like.'

I was lost for words again, I just said a feeble, 'Me too.' I wanted to make love to her then and there—but Gerda passed out.

It was to be a long time before we eventually met up in Paris. I often wondered if she would ever remember that invitation . . .

I had the engine running and took in the ropes at first light. Pete and Gerda slept on. It was a very sheepish Gerda who appeared later. 'I think I must have talked too much last night, Marçel. I don't remember going to bed and getting undressed.'

I gave Gerda my innocent smile. 'I do, Gerda.'

We passed through the locks at Redon after lunch and headed on up the Villane River to Messac where Gerda would be leaving us. We would continue on to Renne the next day to unload the produce. There were several Germans wandering up and down the waterfront.

Pete went into the town to make contact with the Resistance and came back at dusk with two girls. The two young girls came on board and after a few glasses of wine; we were soon enjoying swapping our rather smutty jokes. Later, Pete went off with Gerda and one of the girls. Gerda gave me hug and a kiss that turned my legs to jelly.

I chatted to the other girl until Pete came back to take her home. Gerda was now safely on her way.

Chapter Twelve

We arrived back at Renne at lunchtime the next day. Our cargo of vegetables was immediately unloaded, we swept out the hold and moved over to join the waiting barges where we spent the next few days waiting for our next job. Pete and I spent hours down in the empty hold doing body-building exercises, playing football and cricket.

One morning a German Navy *Leutenant zur See* and an *Obermaat* (NCO) came aboard. 'I wish to inspect your barge to see if it is suitable to take to sea.'

The *Leutenant* spent the next hour carefully going over the barge, looking at the anchor and chain, the hold cover, the state of the hull; and he spent some time in the engine room looking at our fairly new and powerful engine. 'You have a fine barge here, I shall make my report. It is possible we will use you for a special trip across to the Channel Islands.'

Two days later the *Leutenant* turned up with an official document. 'Your barge has been commandeered by the German Navy. You will both be retained as crew. I am *Lieutenant zur See* Hans Shrider and I am taking command of this barge. If you do not cooperate with me entirely you will be removed from the barge. However, if you are cooperative, when this voyage is over, your barge will be returned to you and you will receive one thousand deutschmarks.'

'I see we have little choice, *Herr Leutenant*.'

Pete gave his hand to the Lieutenant. 'If you are reasonable and I must add, good at your job, we will be happy to allow you to run our barge for this trip. My name is Pete and my mate's name is Marçel. You may have a bunk in our cabin.'

'*Sehr goot*, I think you may call me Hans as this is a non-combatant vessel. We will now move over to the main jetty—I will prove to you that I am capable of handling your barge.'

We started the engine, cast off and waited to see what happened. To our surprise and disappointment, Hans handled the barge superbly and brought it alongside the jetty. Two trucks were already there and the *Obermaat* and three sailors were standing to attention.

'Open the hatch cover. We will start work immediately,' Hans called as he jumped ashore. He dismissed the men, the *Obermaat* carried the Lieutenant's kit bag down to the cabin and the three other men started to unload the trucks. I started the winch and pulled back the hatch cover. The Germans passed wooden planks into the hold and began work building a number of partitions. The *Obermaat* was attaching a frame to the bow deck. Later, he fixed a machine gun to the frame.

Another truck arrived with a life raft and a pile of life jackets, which we put on the wheelhouse roof. They erected an aerial on the roof and installed a small transmitter in the wheelhouse. To my disgust, a German Navy flag was hung from the stern of the barge.

By late afternoon, the noise died down. Thirteen stalls had been built at the rear end of the hold. So we were to carry livestock. The Germans and their trucks drove off. 'We stay here tonight. In the morning we move to the jetty where the crane will load our cargo. So tonight, my friends, we have a banquet.'

Hans disappeared ashore and returned much later, his *Obermaat* pulling a laden handcart. *Leutenant* Hans stepped aboard laughing 'Navy supplies my friends, we will certainly not go hungry! Tonight we celebrate my first command in two years. We have plenty of officers but few ships. Karl here will cook us a very good meal tonight. In the meantime…' Hans slapped a bottle of Calvados on the table—and so started a very wild night.

Where the Rance River meets the sea

Strangely enough, I felt little animosity towards Hans; he seemed a different breed. Perhaps being a Navy man and having such a great sense of humour made the difference. As the evening progressed we realised how much he hated the present regime and longed to get back to a peaceful world.

We woke up to find the cabin amazingly clean. Karl had cleaned up and returned to his quarters in the town. After a brew of fresh coffee, Hans moved the barge over to the jetty, which had a small crane.

I thought for a moment we had arrived in the 'Wild West'—six covered wagons were lined up on the jetty, each one pulled by two horses.

Hans was standing next to me. 'It is not a circus, Marçel. The German army is running out of fuel and this is an ideal form of transport for the islands.'

'We could use two of those to pull us down to St Malo and save fuel,' I replied.

'Some fine horse flesh there, Hans, maybe we could stage an accident and fill up our refrigerator,' Pete said laughingly.

The horses were unhitched and taken up the track to a patch of grass. The wagons were loaded with sacks of flour and cartons of foodstuffs. The wheels and covers were removed from the wagons and the crane carefully placed the wagons in the hold, followed by the wheels and covers. Two trucks arrived laden with sacks of flour which were carefully stacked in the hold. The stalls were filled with hay and straw. The horses were brought back and the crane lifted them one by one into the stalls. Karl and his two horse minders put their gear into the last stall. I pulled the hatch cover most of the way over the hold. We had filled up with fuel and water after unloading our last cargo of produce, we were ready to go.

This was a test for all of us, especially for the barge, which had never been to sea. I had very mixed feelings returning to my island homeland. I would not be able to make any form of contact with friends or family.

Chapter Thirteen

hortly after ten on a fine September morning we motored down the Rance. I was steering the barge, we were flying the German Navy flag, carrying German supplies back to my home island, and with a German in command that I could not help liking. Bloody hell!

My hate for the Germans was just as strong, my desire to kill and disrupt was still burning me up. How could we destroy this cargo and these Germans? We were now employed by the enemy.

I would be reluctant to destroy our barge, I would certainly not want to harm all those horses down in the hold and I would be quite sorry to have to kill Hans. I had no desire to contact my family or friends in Jersey, in any case I would be putting them in great danger. For my own safety, I would have to keep out of sight whilst on the island.

Pete joined me in the wheelhouse and for a few minutes we were alone. 'One of fate's little tricks, Marçel. We just have to go along with this for now. Keep your head down when we are in Jersey. You will have to stay on the barge for your own safety. I will take the opportunity of gathering as much information on the island defences as possible.'

'I just hope I can control my frustration without going crazy,' I replied. 'We might get the chance to do something on the way back, Marçel, so just enjoy the trip. You never know, we might even see the RAF boys on the way.'

Pete was quite right so I decided to enjoy the trip; it would be interesting taking our barge across to the island at night.

We were travelling at a steady six knots but because of all the locks we had to pass through, it would take us two days to get to St Malo.

It was dark when we arrived at Hédé. Pete and I decided not to go with the Germans to the café in the village. Instead, we stayed and kept an eye on the horses.

The fortified Isle of Cezembre

We were expected to rendezvous with other barges at St Malo the next evening and we had a long run the next day. We passed the town where I had killed the girl in the back of the truck and which was a short distance from the damaged barges where I had first met Pete and Pierre. In the afternoon, we passed the old town of Dinan and continued down the estuary arriving at Dinard, which is just across the river from St Malo, by evening.

A launch came alongside of us and we were told to tie up to a jetty and be ready to join the other ships at ten pm. At nine, Hans got a message on the radio. We were to move into the centre of the channel where we would be joined by two other barges and a patrol boat. This was a little tricky as there was a strong ebb tide, so we faced the barge upstream with the engine ticking over, in order to remain in the centre of the channel.

At last we saw lights flashing. The patrol boat appeared, followed by two barges. There was just enough light from a half-moon to see the outline of the three other craft. The radio crackled and we were ordered to follow behind the patrol boat ahead of the two other barges. Hans turned our barge around and with full power, we quickly positioned ourselves. This was to be one of the last convoys of barges, as so many barges had been sunk between St Malo and the Channel Islands.

There is a reef about twenty miles long between St Malo and Jersey called des Minquiers. This meant we had to travel a distance of fifty-one nautical miles with a speed of just over six knots. We also had to allow for strong tidal runs and at our speed, it was going to take us at least eight hours to get there.

The sea was relatively calm that night but the Germans

were still kept busy calming the horses. The barges were not designed to travel in rough seas and several had already been lost in storms.

We took two-hour turns at the wheel. Halfway across we got into a swell and it was extremely difficult to keep the barge on a straight course. I had to close the hold completely as the spray was blowing right over the hull. At one stage we lost sight of the patrol boat just at the time we were due to change course. We had left St Malo and were heading northwest. After passing des Minquiers we had to head northeast. Luckily, the patrol boat turned back to find us.

At six the next morning we could see the outline of Jersey. We were now vulnerable to an attack from the air so Karl stood by the machine gun. Twenty minutes later they arrived. Two low-flying aircraft were coming straight for us from astern, firing their guns as they came. The patrol boat and our gun were firing back—Hans spun the wheel and the barge started to turn as one plane flew over us. There were several loud explosions and Pete and I were thrown to the deck—I felt the barge shudder and we were showered with spray. Hans was spinning the wheel again. And then they were gone.

Maybe they were short on fuel. Thanks to Hans and his brilliant timing, we had escaped with just a shower. But the last barge was not so lucky—we could see it sinking, its bow low down in the water.

A message came over the radio. We were to maintain our course and speed whilst the patrol boat picked up the survivors of the sinking barge. We watched the barge disappear under the waves whilst the patrol boat picked up all the survivors.

We followed close behind the patrol boat for the rest of

the way. If there were any stray mines, the patrol boat would be hit first!

With Elizabeth Castle on our left and a reef on our right, we approached the harbour entrance. There were guns pointing from every direction both seaward and skyward and I wondered how close we had passed to mines. I had a funny feeling entering the harbour. Except for the SS *Vega*, a Red Cross ship delivering food parcels to the locals, the harbour seemed deserted. I remembered the times I had played with other kids in small boats, the many gang fights, when we had all finished up wet, tired and happy.

We tied up to the high granite wall of the harbour and Hans and Karl went ashore with the paperwork. I opened up the hold and a crane moved into place. Soon the first of the horses were being lifted out of the hold. Despite the sudden twisting and turning of the barge during the air attack, all the horses had arrived uninjured.

Hans returned with an old camouflaged Morris Minor. 'When we have finished discharging the cargo I will take you around the island in this car.'

I had no inclination to go ashore. 'Hans, I am quite happy to stay here and watch the unloading and then clean up the hold. Why not go off now with Pete. There is so much for you to see.' I could have bitten off my tongue.

Hans looked at me. 'You have been here before?'

I turned away to hide my face. 'No, Hans, but I have read a lot about the island.'

'Let's get going now, Hans. Marçel is right; we have a lot to see.' I knew what he meant. This was a golden opportunity for Pete to gather a lot of information which he would be able to send to London when we arrived back in France. They set off with Karl sitting in the back; I wondered if he was there for a purpose.

The wagons, the flour and food cartons were unloaded and the German sailors, who must have had a very unpleasant journey in the hold (especially when we were attacked from the air), dismantled all the wooden stalls. I got the crane driver to lower a large wooden container, which we filled with all the old straw and horse droppings.

After the last of the Germans had left, I swept out the hold and we were now ready for the next cargo. I had a shower and decided to catch up on some sleep.

I awoke to crashing and banging as the three returned to the barge.

'Wakey, wakey, young Marçel, we are moving across the harbour to a much larger crane. We are to load three army trucks and will return to St Malo tonight. A very interesting tour today, my boy.' Pete had a very satisfied look on his face.

It was after six pm. We moved to the heavy crane and loaded the three trucks and four motorcycles. They completely filled our hold and we were unable to cover the hold as the truck covers were much too high; I just hoped it would be a calm night. The three Germans settled themselves in the rear of one of the trucks.

The second barge, which had carried ammunition, had unloaded and was now loaded with trucks and ready to leave. At nine pm the patrol boat came alongside. We were told to follow close behind the other barge until we were well clear of the island. We would then receive a signal to split up.

The patrol boat was to escort the other barge to the port of Granville and we were to find our own way back to St Malo. Hans was quite happy about this; he had done this trip several times before. He said he knew where the minefields were as he had helped to lay them. I hoped he had a good memory! It was unlikely we would be attacked at night and the weather was good.

We were all standing in the wheelhouse heading for the turning point west of des Minquiers, Hans was at the wheel. 'This war will be soon over my friends. We have some very stupid men in Germany running this war. We have just left the Islands bristling with guns and thousands of our troops manning them. The British will never invade these islands. The local population has its Red Cross food parcels but eventually the Germans will starve. The occupying forces will never harm the locals because they know that one day they will have to surrender to the Allies. The British are laughing because they have thousands of prisoners here and they don't have to feed them.'

'So where does that leave you, Hans?' I wondered if Pete was thinking of taking the barge across to England.

'My friends, I am a German. Because of the heavy losses, boats will no longer be going to the islands. I expect I shall be transferred to the army when the invasion starts and will probably die fighting on land for my doomed country.'

Pete produced the bottle of *Calvados*, grinning. 'Cheers, boys—let's drink to that!' We all enjoyed the joke and the *Calvados*.

By the time we reached the turning point to head towards St Malo, the sea had become rough and we were taking a lot of spray onboard. Water was starting to build up in the open hold. I went below and started up the bilge pump.

A short time later, the sea calmed down and I was able

to stop the pump and I took over the wheel to head south-southeast. Pete and Hans went down into the cabin to brew coffee.

Although it was still dark, I could see a red glow starting to build up in front of us. I called Hans and Pete to come and see. 'My god, St Malo is getting it tonight. I just hope it is all over before daylight as we will be a perfect target for any leftover bombs.'

Hans did not seem too bothered. 'At least the glow will help us find our way up the channel.'

It was just starting to become light when we came abreast of the island of Cezembre—a small island just outside St Malo. It was heavily fortified and with a madman in command, who refused to surrender when St Malo was finally liberated. The island was completely destroyed by Allied bombing.

Fires were burning in several places at St Malo. A launch came out to meet us in the estuary and two officers came aboard. The lock into the basin had been damaged again and we were unable to enter to use the cranes.

This presented a big problem. We would have to wait before we could enter the basin, possibly weeks. As there were no heavy cranes at Dinan or Renne capable of lifting the trucks, we would have to go all the way down to Redon or possibly on to Roche Bernard on the Villane River. It was decided that we would probably be attacked if we stayed here so we were told to make the long trip to Redon. The two sailors went off with the launch and Hans and Kurt remained with us, no doubt to make sure we did'nt steal the trucks!

Late the second day we arrived back at Renne and the following morning set off for Redon. Still unable to unload the trucks at Redon, we continued the next day to Roche Bernard where we were sure there were heavy lifting cranes. This was a crazy situation and demonstrated how inefficient and disorganised the Germans were becoming.

We finally discharged the trucks and Hans and Kurt, to our relief, reluctantly left us while they reported to their headquarters. We had the barge back to ourselves. Unable to destroy or sabotage the trucks, the only benefit from this trip was that later Pete was able to radio a lot of information regarding defences, the health and general state of the Jersey population.

Chapter Fourteen

Pete had received word that the Resistance had an RAF pilot waiting to be flown back to England. His plane had been shot down during an air raid on St Nazaire and he was the sole survivor. The Resistance had watched his parachute descend and had got to him just before the Germans arrived on the scene. He had been taken to a safe house a few miles north of Nantes and was now waiting to be collected.

Our agent had told us we would have to wait a few days before a cargo of produce would be ready for collection at Pontivy. In the meantime he had a load of empty wine casks for us to deliver to Nantes on the Loire River. We loaded up the empty casks and set off for Nantes. On the way we would make our contact with England regarding the pick up of this RAF man.

Due to German infiltration into the Resistance, it was found to be too dangerous for one Resistance group to make direct contact with another, so we acted as a go-between and delivered the airmen to the group that organised the landing strips.

At Redon we entered the canal that ran alongside the Villane River and then headed up the canalised river Isac. It was fifty-seven miles and eighteen locks to Nantes. As soon as we found a quiet spot, we pulled in and Pete went off with the radio, returning two hours later. He had made contact with London and after decoding their reply came up with some surprising news. 'Marçel, the landing point is different this time; in fact it's only a little way ahead from where we are now. Tomorrow night at ten pm we will meet the Resistance two hundred yards east of a road bridge. The road leads on to Plesse, which is close to the Foret du Govre. A replacement for you is arriving and you will return to England with the RAF man.'

I thought about this for a minute. I was reluctant to leave this ideal situation behind but I knew that I needed the training in weapon handling and hand-to-hand fighting; this would enable me to destroy more Germans and be of much more use to Pete.

'That's fine by me, Pete. Just keep this old tub afloat until I get back or else, with all this extra training, I'll beat the hell out of you.' We moved off and fourteen locks later joined the wide and attractive river Erdre. At dusk we finally arrived at Nantes. Nantes is at the lower end of the Loire River and it was extremely busy with many barges of all sizes. We arrived at the jetty where we tied up three abreast. In the morning we would move over to the jetty where we would be unloaded.

'I am going to introduce you to the low life of Nantes tonight, Marçel,' Pete promised.

We crossed over two barges and walked across the road to the café where all the barge men met up with their friends and enemies. They also caught up with their drinking.

We pushed our way through the smoke filled room to the bar. The noise was incredible. At last the *patron* came over to us and gave Pete a warm handshake, they exchanged a few words and he produced two glasses of red wine and nodded his head in the direction of the table at the end of the bar. We pushed and shoved our way over to the table and sat down with the two men sitting there. One man got up and left. Pete leant over and spoke quietly to the other man. '*Comment vous appelez vous?*'

The pale faced man looked very out of place amongst all us weather beaten barge men. He whispered, 'Flying Officer John McDonald at your service, sir, and already to go, old boy.' I thought it was hardly the time to be so flippant.

As we started to get up, the doors of the café flew open and several *Feldgendamerie* burst in. The café was suddenly silent. The Germans moved forward, examining identity cards.

I noticed the *patron* give a signal to a large rough-looking man leaning on the bar. This man picked up his glass and threw it at Pete hitting him on the side of his head. Pete picked up a bottle off the table, smashed the end off and rushed at the man at the bar—and then all hell was let loose.

A fight to end all fights started, the Germans stood stunned. They backed away to the door and watched as we tried to beat hell out of each other—chairs, glasses and bottles were flying in all directions, the screams and shouts must have been heard for miles around as old scores were settled.

I dragged myself off the floor with the taste of blood in my mouth and was grabbed by the *patron* who had come around the bar. He pushed me and John McDonald through the door to the toilets; at the end of the passage way he unlocked a door and shoved us both out into a side alley. The door slammed behind us.

I had to get the Flying Officer back to our barge and the safety of the tank. We crept to the end of the lane, I told John to keep close behind me. Truckloads of Germans were arriving. We crept along the side of the building and away from the café. I could see a stack of empty crates on the jetty a little way ahead. We slipped across the road and got behind the crates. The *Feldgendamerie* were bringing the now-subdued customers out of the café and loading them into the trucks. I wondered where Pete was; if he had been arrested I would have to take command and deliver John to the aircraft. I realised I would have to stay behind to take charge of the barge and not fly to England.

Germans started moving in our direction. 'Follow me, John. I hope you can swim. This is our only way back to the barge.'

He seemed to be enjoying himself. 'Like a fish, old boy. Lead on!'

I was not in the mood for his frivolous humour, 'Just shut up, John, and follow me.'

We jumped down onto the deck of the barge in front of us and quietly stepped across the other two. 'Take off your boots and jacket and follow me.'

We dropped into the water on the outer side of the barge

and swam until we arrived at the next line of barges. I was pretty sure our barge was in the next line. When we got to our barge we could hear voices and there were lights flashing inside the cabin. Our barge was being searched.

We moved right under the stern and clung to the rudder. After a while, the Germans moved on. We waited a few minutes and then climbed aboard. I gave John some dry clothes. He dried himself whilst I made some hot coffee. I took him as well as all the wet clothes down to the tank. I showed him where everything was and told him to fasten the tank entrance plate once he was in and not to make any noise. Back on deck the Germans were still searching barges. I wondered how many of the barge men had been taken to prison. There was nothing I could do, so I climbed into my bunk and eventually fell asleep.

When I woke at first light, there was no sign of Pete. He had shown me where we were expected to unload our cargo, so I decided to move the barge across on my own. I started the engine, untied the ropes and carefully reversed out into the middle of the canal. Because we were in a wide part of the basin I was able to turn the barge around and move over to the other side where we were due to unload. The agent came and collected the paperwork. Shortly after, the empty casks were unloaded, and then we were loaded with full casks of wine.

I took some coffee and a sandwich down to John and warned him that he would have to stay there until we got moving later in the morning. I was just deciding what to do next when a German motor cycle and sidecar came bumping down the road to the jetty. Pete was sitting in it, looking very pleased with himself.

Pete climbed out and handed the German something, he turned the motor cycle around and drove off.

'How much did that cost you, Pete?'

'A lot more than what you're worth, Marçel. I was quite determined I would get rid of you tonight and let the Army boys in England sort you out.'

We compared injuries. Pete had a bad cut on the side of his face and a very puffy nose whilst I had a black eye and swollen lips. I started the engine, reversed the barge and we moved off.

'I really don't understand how you manage to persuade the Germans to do these things for you, Pete.' Pete put his hand in his pocket and showed me several blank gold coins. 'This my boy. This is a very persuasive language. The morale of the average German at present is pretty low, they have a good idea where Germany is heading and they will go on fighting to the end, but they realise that the war is nearly over and gold is the only thing that will help them survive.'

Pete took over the wheel. 'Last night, Marçel, was a classic example. The Germans at the café were not *Gestapo*. They held back whilst we beat each other up and then rounded us all up and took us down to the prison. The Germans need the boat people, so when the *patron* from the café produced a few of these coins, we were all sent home to face the wrath of our wives and sweethearts. However if they had found the RAF, boy it might have been a completely different story. Speaking of which, he could come up for a while.'

Flying Officer John McDonald was much relieved at coming out of the tank and tucked enthusiastically into our cooked breakfast. We had ten miles of the wide and beautiful Erdre River before we entered the first canal and we expected to arrive at our meeting point at about nine pm.

I had mixed feelings about leaving the barge. Seeing the last aeroplane a ball of fire didn't do much for my self confidence. I put all my things in a bag under my bunk except for my friend the bayonet, which was now part of me anyway and which I might possibly still need tonight.

It was almost dark when we arrived at the rendezvous. We tied up to a derelict jetty and waited. At ten, two well-armed Resistance men appeared. One was to stay and guard the barge until Pete got back. He would warn Pete in case the Germans discovered the barge.

We set off with the other Resistance man, Pete and I each carried a Sten gun. We walked in single file; I followed a little way behind as rear guard. We walked for an hour without incident along a dirt track until we reached the forest. By now we could hear planes overhead and the rumbling in the distance of the bombs that were falling on St Nazaire.

Arriving at a road that ran at right angles to our track, we were met by another Resistance man. He signalled us to turn right and follow the road. The trees had been cut back on both sides of it, presumably as a fire break for the forest. The road was quite wide at this point.

We were met by yet another man, who told us to wait by the side of the road. A few minutes later we heard the sound of vehicles approaching. We crouched down in the long grass. The convoy of trucks passed by and then we heard the sound of our aircraft overhead.

I don't know how the Resistance had managed this timing, but from somewhere ahead we heard loud explosions coming from the convoy of trucks followed by a lot of gunfire.

The *Lysander* landed on the road just in front of us. I embraced Pete, handed him the Sten gun and then ran with John to the aircraft. As we reached it a man jumped out—my replacement. We scrambled in, the plane was moving off as we closed the door. John fixed my safety belt and we were airborne.

Looking down I could see the trucks on fire. I hoped Pete would get back to the barge safely and then move on, well away from this area.

To the left I could see a large red glow coming from St Nazaire. It must be hell there at the moment; I hoped the U-boat pens were being demolished.

This was my first flight in an aircraft and I was not frightened, just excited at the prospect of arriving in England. We were joined by two other aircraft, one on each side. I could see their exhaust flames and it was comforting to know we had an escort. Looking down I could see water. We were crossing the channel.

Dawn was breaking as we approached the south coast of England. I could just make out the faint outline of the coast. The two other aircraft dropped away, we were now on our own. I could feel the pressure on my ears as we started to descend. We made a very bumpy landing on the grass runway just outside Exeter, and taxied across to some buildings. It was now quite light.

The pilot jumped out and helped us climb out from the back seats. 'Enjoy the trip chaps? At least I don't have to clean up any vomit this time. Anyway welcome to England.'

Chapter Fifteen

A jeep with an officer and driver pulled up alongside the aircraft. The army captain shook hands all around, the pilot and John walked off to the control tower and I scrambled into the back of the jeep. The captain sat in front with the driver, we passed out through the airfield checkpoint and drove for about an hour.

The countryside was quite different to Brittany. We were somewhere on the moors when we finally reached a large army camp. We drove through a maze of Nissan huts and eventually pulled up outside of one.

An army sergeant was waiting for us and the three of us went into the hut. There was a small room just inside the door, the NCO's quarters; a line of beds as yet not occupied filled the rest of the hut. A door at the bottom end of the hut led to the washrooms.

'I am Captain Norton and will be responsible for your training and all your needs whilst you are here. Sergeant Bennet will very soon make a man out of you—that's if you survive his training course. You will be joined by fourteen other men in the next few days. You will be undergoing an officers' training course, which I assure you is tough. After this, you will continue on a special training course that has been specifically designed for you. This will run for several months, at the end of which you might possibly receive a commission.'

I took an immediate liking to Captain Norton. He was cheerful and friendly but as I was soon to find out—very tough and ruthless. I was to see a lot of him in the next few months.

'I'm told your code name is Piglet; it has been decided that whilst you are training in England you will assume the name of Simon Phillips. Welcome to Britain, Simon. I understand you have already seen far more action than a lot of us. I must say I was expecting someone a little older. Sergeant Bennet will take you for your medical and will get you fixed up with kit. After that, I suggest you get some food and sleep. Be ready to be escorted to your interrogation at six pm. Any questions? If you have any problems come directly to me.'

The jeep moved off with Captain Norton, and I was left with the sergeant. 'Right, young man, your kit is all ready on your bunk, the toilets and washroom are through that door at the end of the hut. Get yourself cleaned up and when you get back, put on this battle dress and the boots and I will take you across for your medical and after that to the canteen for some food. We can always change your boots if they don't fit.'

I nearly froze to death under the cold shower but that was nothing to the cold I was to experience in the next few months.

I was surprised to find how well the uniform fitted and the heavy boots were just right for me.

'Stand up straight, boy, and follow me.' Sergeant Bennet marched me to the medical centre where I gave my age as seventeen. I received a full medical examination and was passed as extremely fit. I had certainly changed in the last few months—I had grown to five foot eight, weighed eleven stone, shaved every day, and had a strong sex drive.

We crossed over to the canteen where I lined up in the queue. That first breakfast of bacon and eggs was the best I have ever tasted, then I was marched back to my hut and spent the rest of the day catching up on sleep.

At five-thirty pm, I was taken over to the camp headquarters and at six, entered the room where I was to be interrogated.

I was reminded of the interrogation back in St Helier.

I sat on a chair opposite three officers who sat behind tables; Captain Norton was one of them. Once again I had a strong light focused on me—I was not impressed.

The senior officer, who looked old and rather pompous, addressed me, 'Private Phillips. We are here to establish who you are, your background, and the all events leading up to your arrival in England. We will then decide if you are a suitable person to receive the benefit of our special training. We expect absolute respect and obedience from you whilst you are here. Any breach of our rules, because of your background, and you will be sent to a prison for the rest of the war.'

We had started on a bad note and I could feel the anger rising inside of me. This was not what I had expected and I had not come to England to be addressed in that way. I stood up straight.

'Sir, I have come here from France to improve my ability to harass and kill as many Germans as possible. I expect to return to France as soon as I have received your expert training. Yes, I will respect and obey you all whilst I am here, but Sirs, I am here of my own free will and I expect equal respect from you. I will certainly not allow myself to be threatened. I have done and will be doing far more for the Allied cause than a lot of you people. In the last few months I have seen good people killed, and in return I have killed several Germans. That you should address me in such terms when you need people like me working for you in France is absurd.'

I sat down exhausted. I had even surprised myself.

I detected a smile on the faces of the other two men but the senior officer was suppressing his anger. 'I am sure we will overcome any differences. You will be treated fairly. You are quite right, you are a volunteer and we do owe you the respect you deserve. However this establishment is run on very strict lines and we expect you to follow them.'

Then followed a string of questions regarding my background, my family and the events leading up to my meeting with Pierre. I had to give details of each of my killings and the suicide of *Oberleutenant* Grossman. Luckily, through Pete's report, they had already been informed of most of these events, otherwise I think it might have been hard for them to believe my story.

Three hours later, I was dismissed; Captain Norton followed me out. 'Come with me, Phillips.' I followed him into his office and an attendant brought in some hot coffee.

'You did well tonight. Some of our senior officers, especially those that have come out of retirement, have not adjusted too well to the methods we now adopt in the Services. Tonight you have gained the respect you deserve.' He leaned back in his chair. 'I have met both Pete and Pierre. You have been associated with two good men. They must have realised your worth.'

I sipped my coffee. 'I got on well with both of them, Sir, I consider Pete a good friend and the last I saw of Pierre he was hanging from a tree.'

Captain Norton was silent for a while. 'I trained his wife. Gerda is a very courageous woman. Poor woman, I hope she survives the war.'

Somehow, I found my way back to my Nissan hut. The sergeant was reading in his room.

The next morning was chaotic as the fourteen other recruits moved in. They were all several years older than me and had already done their initial training.

I was once again thrown into a completely different world; the next six months were spent drilling, marching, handling weapons and hand to hand fighting. I learnt to drive heavy trucks, handle explosives and was shown how to kill at close quarters, this I already knew. At night and at weekends when all the other men were relaxing, I was given tuition in French, German, Portuguese and to my astonishment, a little information about wine making.

This was the toughest time of my life; I was transformed from a gangling youth to a tough soldier. The hard physical training kept my mind alert so that, despite the tiredness, I was able to absorb the language lessons that I received in the evenings. I trained myself to sleep from five-thirty pm to six-thirty. After a meal I would study until eleven, I then slept on until six am.

On Christmas Eve I was told to report to Captain Norton.

'I am going to my farm in Hampshire for two days; my wife, children and I would like you to join us.' I was delighted. I had not been outside the camp, except on exercises, since arriving in England. The thought of spending Christmas with a family was an unexpected pleasure. 'Grab your toothbrush. We leave in one hour.'

We set off in a jeep. I was the Captain's official driver and this was my first opportunity to see a bit of England. We drove through Exeter and Taunton to a lovely old village near Glastonbury and stopped outside the village inn. This was my first time in an old pub with low ceilings, panelled walls and stone floor. It was lunchtime and the bar was filled mostly with locals and just a few RAF men. The Captain was greeted by several of the locals. The place was filled with chatter and laughter, it was Christmas and they had started celebrating.

Mine host greeted the Captain, 'When are you going to cross the Channel, Bill? If this goes on much longer Britain will start to sink with the weight of all these Americans.' He placed two overflowing pints of beer in front of us.

I suddenly realised I didn't have any English money. No one had thought of giving me any and as I had no need for money in the camp, it had not entered my mind.

'Sir, I don't have any money to buy you a beer, I only have a few Reich marks which I'm sure would not go down too well in this pub.'

'Good god, man, so you haven't. It never crossed my mind, as you are not officially in the army it has been completely overlooked. I will definitely fix that up when we return. In the meantime take this as a loan.' He handed me five pounds, which seemed like a fortune to me.

'Let's go, Private Phillips, my wife Sophie will be waiting for us and I'm dying to see her and the kids, it's been three weeks since I last saw them.

We were met at the cottage door by Sophie, a very attractive brunette. She was quite small and had a lovely figure, she reminded me of an older version of Simone. Sophie threw herself at the Captain. When he finally put her down, she turned to me and gave me a light kiss on the cheek. 'And who have we here, Bill, I see you've brought me a lovely young man for Christmas.'

'Let's drop the formalities whilst we are at home. Sophie this is Simon. Simon this is Sophie and I'm Bill, until we get back to the camp, Simon. My kids are Buddha and Chips—officially Jennifer and Peter. Chips was the first word Jennifer uttered and it's pretty obvious why we call Peter the Buddha.'

The front door opened directly into a charming living room, Chips was sitting in a playpen surrounded by her toys. She gave me a beautiful 'come on' smile. Buddha smiled at me from his pram; I was reminded of the laughing Buddha.

We spent the afternoon playing with the children and decorating a Christmas tree with lights. After high tea, I went up to the small box room where I was to sleep. Sophie did everything possible to make me feel at home; I had almost forgotten what family life was like!

Later when the children had been put to bed we sat around a cosy log fire and discussed the state of the war. Bill had left his father to run the farm when he joined the army, and was itching to get back as soon as the war ended. I started to feel uneasy talking about peace; I had my own internal war to fight and had enjoyed killing. How would I ever be able to control the power I had, to be able kill a man without feeling any remorse? I had now committed myself to maybe several years of eliminating escaping Nazis. Where was this leading? Could I ever stop killing—would I ever be a normal person again?

My thoughts were interrupted by a loud banging on the front door. Bill opened the door and gasped, 'Good God. What the hell are you doing here?'

He stepped aside to let the visitor in. 'Tracked you down, old boy, how are you? Actually I've come to pick up the 'Piglet'; we have a job to do tomorrow.'

Pete came across to the fireplace and gave Sophie a big hug. 'Pete, how lovely to see you after all this time—I hope you are going to spend Christmas with us.'

'Sorry, Sophie old dear, I'm here to take your guest away.' He turned to me, gave me a quick embrace. 'Marçel, old boy, I need you for a few days. I have a suitcase with some suitable civilian clothes for you; we have to report to the RAF at Dunkeswell by six pm tomorrow.'

Sophie took Pete's arm. 'Pete dear, you must stay the night, we'll have an early Christmas lunch and you can easily make Dunkeswell by five.'

Peter was delighted with the idea. Bill went and fetched a girl from next door to come and baby-sit and the four of us set off to the pub.

After a hilarious evening, we returned to the cottage, all a lot worse for wear. Pete and I squeezed into the box room, collapsed onto the bunks and promptly fell asleep.

We woke up to the delicious smell of cooking. Sophie was

preparing lunch. By the time we got ourselves together and I had dressed in a shirt and tie, supplied by Pete, it was time for lunch. After real Christmas fare of turkey, Christmas pudding and all the trimmings, Bill produced a bottle of Port wine, which we finished between us.

We made our reluctant farewells and set off in Pete's red sports car to Dunkeswell. It was raining all the way and dark when we arrived at the Air Base. We went into the office that was under the control tower where several other well-dressed civilians were waiting. Outside I could just make out the outline of a *Lancaster* bomber, only it was not camouflaged but appeared to be peacetime silver.

I was unable to contain my curiosity any longer, 'Where are we going, Pete?'

Pete tried to look casual and stifled a yawn. 'Porto in Portugal, old boy!'

I tried not to be impressed and waited for Pete to continue. He remained silent. A Flight Sergeant came in and advised us to go to the toilet, as there were no such luxuries on our aircraft, and that we would soon be departing.

He was certainly right. The inside of the fuselage was unlined and you could see the cables that ran down the sides of it, which controlled the tail end. There was a row of seats running down each side. We each had a seat belt and a blanket—this was to prove necessary when the aircraft climbed up into the cold air.

When we took off, the noise was deafening and we just sat there as the hours slowly went by, sleep was impossible.

Eventually we heard the engines slow down and my ears started to pop as we descended, and eventually, after several heavy bumps, landed. So much for the glamour of flying! The sun was well up and we were in for a fine but cool day.

We spent some time with immigration but as we only had a small amount of hand luggage, we quickly passed through customs.

We were met by a smartly dressed man who spoke quite good English who introduced himself as Alfonso Baidassaris and ushered us into his equally smart Renault saloon and we set off heading south.

'Gentlemen, I think I have found the perfect property for you. The main buildings consist of an old renovated castle, which is right on the side of a deep river. This river runs into the large inland waterway and from which you may gain access to the ocean.' He paused to negotiate several sharp bends in the road and continued.

'The property includes a very large acreage of vines. Before the war the people who ran this estate dispatched regular supplies of their excellent wine to Northern France and Germany.'

Pete leaned forward. 'So why is it all up for sale now, Alfonso?'

'The war my friends. The wine used to be delivered by road, a long slow process. When the war started it became impossible to continue and after three years the winery had to close down and the owners went bankrupt.'

We were now travelling along a straight road; the country around us was quite low lying with a number of streams and wetlands.

'Alfonso, what happened to all the staff at the winery? Are they still about?' I could see Pete was becoming quite enthusiastic.

'Most of the workers moved on but the original 'Wine Master' is still there; he and his wife are the caretakers of the property.' Alfonso gave us a lot more details of the property and the surrounding area. After a while, we found we were driving alongside a large estuary where several rivers converged before eventually reaching the ocean. We turned left off the main road and crossed a small bridge and then turned right, down a narrow road until we came to an imposing entrance— we had arrived at the property. The track continued through acres of vines, they all looked neglected and sometimes were hidden by the tall weeds, in the distance we could see an area of trees, and rising above the trees, the old castle.

We drove through an archway into the courtyard. On three sides were buildings where the wine was made and stored, and on the fourth side an imposing building, which was the owner's residence. The wine master and his wife were waiting at the large studded front door to greet us when we got out of the car.

Alfonso introduced us to José and Maria, his wife. They were both in their fifties, José was able to speak a little English and they seemed very happy to see us. I had a feeling we would get on well with this couple.

José gave us a tour of the house whilst Maria went off to prepare lunch. It was an impressive entrance hall with a superb wide wooden stairway, leading up to the bedrooms. Upstairs, a passageway ran the length of the back of the building. It had several skylights, as the back wall was part of the old castle wall. There were six bedrooms and three bathrooms. They were all fine rooms but the whole house was run down and needed to be completely redecorated.

On the ground floor along one side of the hallway, double

doors led into a large lounge and then an archway through to the library. A door then led on to the study or office. The office had access to the courtyard. On the other side of the hallway there was a large dining room and beyond that, the kitchen and staff rooms.

Maria had prepared a superb lunch for us. She produced an enormous baked fish with a surprising assortment of fresh vegetables. José fetched some bottles, which he carefully opened. It was a very pleasant light white wine, which was his pride and joy.

After lunch we inspected the outbuildings where the wine was made and eventually bottled and then down to the cellars where the rows and rows of casks were stored.

'We still have a lot of good wine in store. This will be ready to sell when the war ends, but there is also a considerable amount that is now only fit to dump.' José gave a sigh, thinking of all the hard work gone to waste. 'It will take two seasons to get the vines back into production, but as we still have a lot of wine to sell, we can quickly get back into business. I know that because of the long rest time, some of the more recent plantings will produce much improved wine.'

We piled into an old truck and José took us on a tour of the vinery. It extended for miles around but we could see there was a tremendous amount of work needed to clean up the vines before they became productive again.

It was dark when at last we got back to the castle, José produced a bottle of his sherry, I could see it was going to be a long night.

The four of us retired to the office. 'What do you think, Marçel? Do you think this would suit our purposes?'

I nodded my head enthusiastically. 'Yes, providing we are able to take a boat out to the ocean.'

Pete turned to José. 'José, would you and your wife be prepared to work for us, you as wine master and your wife as housekeeper?'

José was smiling. 'We have always hoped that one day we would be able to bring this great vinery back into production.'

Pete continued, 'We intend to run the vinery as a successful business. We are also working for a Government agency that is helping to rid Europe of certain undesirable people. Our job is to bring them here and to then take them out to a ship that will transport them on to a country in South America. This country is prepared to accept them.'

Pete paused and gave José a piercing look. 'This would mean you and Maria would be working in absolute secrecy with regard to this matter.'

José remained silent for a minute. 'My wife and I would not want to be involved in anything illegal. We would be happy to run the vinery and the house for you. What you do after that is entirely your own business. We would not be involved in anything other than running the vinery, and as your servants, would be absolutely discreet and loyal to you.'

Pete looked satisfied and leaned forward eagerly. 'We would want you to start bringing the vines back into production now. The house would need to be completely redecorated to accommodate us and our guests.'

José was delighted. 'Sir, you will have no regrets, Maria and I will be delighted to serve you and we will be so very happy to bring this vinery back to its old glory. We will need to engage some of the old workers and of course it will need a fair bit of money to restore everything.'

'José, go and talk to Maria now and make sure she is happy with our arrangements and is prepared to be our housekeeper.' José shook both our hands and almost ran out of the room to tell Maria the news.

We spent the next few hours discussing the details. Pete made Alfonso an offer well below the asking price, after a somewhat heated argument, Alfonso accepted the offer on behalf of his clients, the bank. After arranging to pick us up early afternoon the next day, he set off to the bank to inform them of the sale of the property.

Later, José appeared with a bottle of Madeira and we discussed in detail the improvements that we wished to make to the house and the work that had to be done to the vinery. Eventually Maria came and collected us. She had prepared a delicious meal of roast duck.

'José, do you think you could organise a boat trip for us in the morning?' Pete asked. 'We would quite like to see how far it is to the ocean entrance from here.'

José walked over to the phone. 'My brother has a motor boat. I will ask him to pick us up from our jetty in the morning.' He put the phone down. 'He will be with us at nine am and will take you to the entrance and back. He has a fine fishing boat.' It had been a long day with no sleep the night before so we decided to make use of the cold and uninviting bedrooms.

A door in the castle wall led from the courtyard to the jetty. We stood on the jetty and watched the motor boat approaching. The river here was about fifteen yards wide and looked quite deep. The boat came alongside, we jumped aboard, José introduced us to his brother and we set off down the river.

About two miles down, the river ran into the estuary. I was surprised how well the channels were marked. The estuary was wide with several small islands. It looked an ideal place for a boating holiday. We followed the channel for an hour and arrived at the entrance; this was a tidal area and I could imagine it would be very difficult to exit in stormy conditions.

As we went out through the entrance, I saw a small village on one side and dunes on the other, there was quite a swell and the tide was running fast. Once out in the ocean, it was a clear run to Porto to the north or Lisbon to the south. We headed back to the estuary riding the swell as we passed back through the entrance.

'This is perfect; we have deep water all the way from the castle to the ocean. We could bring a large ship through here without any problem.' Pete was delighted. I could see our plans were taking shape.

After lunch, Alfonso arrived with the paperwork for us to sign. The bank had accepted Pete's offer and the castle would soon be ours.

'Alfonso will take you back to the airport, Marçel.' I will stay on here and to tie things up, and then I will try to organise the transport from here to northern France. I will meet up with you in about three month's time. I expect the invasion of France will take place early next summer. Thanks to all our hard work, the French Resistance is now so strong, I believe they will be taking over a large part of Brittany in the spring.'

I shook hands warmly with José and Maria and gave Pete a hug. 'You can look after my car until I get back, Marçel. Try not to wreck it.' We set off for the airport. It had been a most interesting Christmas.

The night flight back to England was just as uncomfortable and boring. We arrived at Dunkeswell at dawn—it was raining heavily. I found the red sports car and drove back to the army camp on the moors. It was still raining; I changed back into my uniform and reported to Captain Norton who had also returned that morning. I thanked him for their hospitality. I think he knew where I had been but said nothing. He told me where I could safely park Pete's car. The holiday was over and discipline resumed.

The next three months were pretty tough but by April, I was able to speak French and German quite well, I could handle any type of weapon and drive every possible type of vehicle. I was one hundred per cent fit and itching to return to France.

Chapter Sixteen

I t was towards the end of April when I was ordered to go to Exeter airport. Pete was waiting there for me. After a warm greeting, he laughingly examined his car for any scratches. 'Something very interesting has turned up in France, Marçel. We are going back tonight but first we have to meet my boss which is a fair distance from here.'

We set off in Pete's red bombshell and arrived at Ashmore Manor at midday. We were immediately ushered into Stephen Harvey's office.

'Good to see you, Pete, so this is our infamous 'Piglet'. Sorry about that, welcome to our club, Marçel, I'm afraid it is going to be short lived, as you and Pete are to be killed off when you return to France tonight.' Stephen indicated to us to sit down. 'Seriously, the time has come for you to disappear. We want the Resistance to believe you are dead so that you can prepare yourselves for your next operation, which is operation 'Deserting Rats.'

Pete was grinning. 'How do want us to die, Stephen? I hope it will be quick and painless!'

Stephen leaned back in his chair. 'I have one last job for you in France, Pete. I expect you are wondering why I asked you to take a barge load of gravel and cement to Pontivy.' Stephen smiled at Pete's look of horror.

'No not that Pete—something very interesting has turned up. We have been informed that three U-boats have been holed up in a creek on the Blavet tidal estuary. We understand the torpedo tubes have been removed and trucks are entering the compound loaded with crates that we believe are stolen art treasures.'

Stephen had us both sitting up—this sounded interesting.

Stephen continued, 'We have known for some time that the 'King Rats' would want to take their nest eggs to South America. This looks like an opportunity for us to save some of these precious items from disappearing forever.'

'We believe the French Resistance will be taking over the whole of Brittany in the next few months so we need to delay the escape of these U-boats until that time.' Stephen leaned forward.

'I want you to fly back to Brittany tonight. We will drop you, and a batch of explosives, which the Resistance boys will deliver to your barge. I want them to watch you all the way; you will go down the Blavet canal in time to arrive at the Blavet estuary just before dusk. About a mile down the estuary on the right hand side you will see some camouflaged netting and behind that a lock gate. Make sure that you have your explosives well placed, bow and stern. When you hit the lock gates, you press the firing button—you will have forty-five seconds to get as far away as possible from the explosion. I want the Resistance to believe you died there.'

Pete was not smiling.'So this is where we get killed, Stephen. Forty-five seconds to get away? Not easy; I need smoke bombs to go off just ahead of the explosives. We will have to swim up the estuary and land on the same side, as the Resistance boys will be watching from the opposite bank. Good; if we get that far, then I have no worries about getting away and travelling to Paris and then across to northern France. The Germans are far too occupied preparing for the invasion and fighting the Resistance.'

After a little more discussion we shook hands and left and drove back to Exeter airport both deep in thought. I was thinking of Churchill's words. Was this to be the end of the beginning or the beginning of the end? We stopped off in Exeter for fish and chips and arrived at the airfield at seven pm.

As usual Pete was able to produce suitable bargemen's clothes from his suitcase, and then to my horror I was told we would be landing by parachute. I had done some training at jumps and landings and we had all made one actual parachute jump from an aircraft, but that was in daylight. We were both fitted with a parachute and instructed to count to five before pulling the cord that opened the chute. Pete slapped me on the shoulder. 'Don't worry, Marçel, we will bail out north of Pontivy. You should see the canal from the air. When you land if you can't find me, look for the canal and then head south until you get to Pontivy. We'll meet up on the barge.'

Our aircraft took off at ten pm. I was feeling sick, worried about a night landing. What if I landed in a tree or in the canal? At last I felt a tap on my shoulder. Pete was shouting in my ear, 'Time for little pigs to fly.'

I stood by the open door frozen with fear—the pilot raised his hand and Pete gave me a push—I was out in space and I forgot to count, then I started to count but thought this ridiculous so I pulled the cord and felt a heavy jerk on my shoulders, then I breathed a sigh of relief. A little way ahead, I could see Pete's parachute and the canal on my left. My euphoria didn't last long. I saw the trees rising up towards me. I braced myself and fell in a heap between the trees. I quickly released myself and pulled in and folded the parachute. I found a large bush and stuffed it out of sight.

Pete must have been quite some distance from me so firstly I had to find the canal. It had been on my left side as I descended but I had spun around several times since then. I heard the distant rumbling and could see a pink glow in the distance. That would be an air raid at Lorient to the west. I headed south.

I soon came to the canal and followed it until I arrived at Pontivy. I crept cautiously past some buildings until I arrived at the jetty. There was someone onboard. I edged around the outside of the cabin until I could see through a porthole. Pete was making coffee.

We sat silently for a while. 'I hope that was a once in a lifetime, Pete. Thanks for the push. For a moment I was just unable to move.'

'Some people do it for pleasure, Marçel. We were both lucky tonight not to break anything. You will find a big change here since last year. The Germans mostly stay in their barracks, unable to cope with the now powerful French Resistance. This means we will be able to travel more freely.'

There was a thump on the deck. The Resistance men had delivered the explosives. They dropped them in the wheelhouse and quietly left. We placed most of them down in the chain locker in the bow of the barge and the rest in the engine room close to the stern of the barge. It was starting to get light and I felt it was time to move.

'Let's get going, Pete. There should be someone at the first lock by the time we get there.'

We started the engine, untied the ropes and moved out. We had thirty-seven miles and twenty-eight locks to the Blavet estuary. It was not possible to make it in one day as it would be dark well before we reached the estuary. We had to find a safe spot for the night and we could not risk being searched with all the explosives we carried on the barge.

By early afternoon we were passing through a forest when we spotted a small creek. We turned the barge and slowly moved through the reeds and water lilies until we found a spot under the overhanging trees. We were completely out of sight from the river.

Pete and I spent the rest of the day fixing detonators to the explosives and running cables back to the wheelhouse. Stephen had supplied us with smoke bombs which we attached to both sides of the barge By evening we were both ready to catch up on our lack of sleep the night before.

Next morning we checked over our work and were satisfied that the barge would be destroyed forty five seconds after we pressed the button. There would be no second chance.

'This might be a good place to leave our gear; it's a fair distance from our destination, which is good, because after the explosion we will have to move fast. We need to be unencumbered with our packs.' Pete agreed.

We walked through the forest until we came to an outcrop of rock. From the top of this rock we were able to see that the forest extended for miles in both directions. We could see no sign of habitation. 'Excellent. On the way back we can keep the canal in sight and this outcrop is a perfect landmark. Let's get our gear, Pete, and conceal it at the foot of the hill.'

We packed a change of clothes, some food, the Sten guns and revolvers, a few hand grenades and water bottles in our packs and concealed them in a crevice at the bottom of the outcrop.

After a good lunch and a bottle of red wine, we set off on our last journey with the barge. It had been our home and the base from which we had been able to achieve so much.

The light was fading when we passed through the last of the locks; we had only a short way to go to reach our target on the right bank. We slipped into shorts and tied our shoes to our belts. We were wearing only light shirts and were both shivering, partly from cold but mostly excitement. We were travelling at half speed when I spotted some camouflaged netting. As we got closer we could see the lock gates. Pete and I shook hands. 'We'll meet up at the creek, Marçel. Good luck, old boy, and don't be late!'

With the engine at full speed, Pete turned the barge and headed straight for the lock gates. It was almost dark now and we were travelling at full speed ahead. We were now very close—as we approached the lock gates head-on Pete fired off the smoke bombs; locked the steering wheel and pressed the firing button 'GO! NOW!'

I dived off the stern being careful to keep well clear of the propeller. It seemed ages before I surfaced—all I could see was black smoke and then a deafening crash as the barge hit the lock gates followed by the ear shattering explosion. I saw an enormous red flash through the smoke and then I was hit by the shock waves—I swam as hard as I could to get away from the flames that were lighting up the sky, burning bits of debris were falling in the water around me. Suddenly it became very quiet, the barge had settled on the bottom and the flames extinguished. I could hear a siren screaming and Germans shouting and yelling. I kept swimming as fast as I could back up the river; I wondered if Pete had got away in time.

The smoke and the darkness enabled me to get well away, unseen by the Germans. I kept going for about thirty minutes and then climbed up the bank and rested where it was very quiet. I could not resist going back to see if we had been successful. The tide was low so I crept along the narrow beach until I came to a fence that ran down to the water.

A guard was standing on top of the bank. I waited. As soon as he moved off I slipped down into the water and around the fence. I was in the compound. I moved along a small beach at the bottom of the bank and came to a wall. There was no sign of a guard so I climbed onto the wall and was able to look down on the entrance to the canal. Floodlights were shining down on the lock gates, which had been completely blown inwards. They appeared irreparable. I could just make out part of the bow of the barge stuck in between the two damaged gates; the rest of the barge was under water.

I slipped down off the wall and crept back the way I had come. No sign of the guard. They evidently were not expecting a second visit that night. As soon as I was well clear of the fence, I broke into a fast walk as I had a long way to go to our meeting point. Our attack had been completely successful— the cement would set on top of the gravel. It would take a long time to clear the canal. The U-boat was safely locked in behind our barge.

My training of the last six months was paying off; I was able to keep up a steady pace for most of the night. I kept well clear of all the lock gates but stayed most of the time within sight of the canal. It was dawn when I eventually arrived at the rock face. I was just about to reach into the crevice to retrieve our pack when I felt cold steel pressing into my neck.

'Getting a little careless aren't we. Why have you been so long?' I felt stupid—I had just broken a golden rule and could have easily walked into a trap.

'That was stupid of me, Pete. Definitely won't be repeated. I went back to see the damage. The gates were completely destroyed and the barge perfectly placed to seal off the entrance.'

We were both feeling elated and relieved that we had come out unscathed from the event. 'The Resistance were waiting for us on the other side of the estuary. They will assume we were blown up with the barge. Marçel, you and I are now dead.'

We decided to rest up for the day. We climbed to the top of the rock and took it in turns to catch up on sleep.

Later in the day, we ate some of our food and discussed our future plans. We were now partners in a business, with a large vinery in Portugal to run. Our war in Brittany was over and we were now going to conduct a business that in some ways would be far more dangerous than anything that we had done so far.

Our biggest problem for now would be avoiding the French

Resistance; the last thing they would want would be to see German war criminals being helped to escape, with their gold, to Portugal.

Because of our sponsors, we would not be able to reveal the fact that these people were to be eventually killed and dumped at sea. Our enterprise would only succeed if we were able to maintain complete secrecy. We had no illusions—if our activities came to light, our sponsors would not hesitate to remove us from the face of the earth to avoid embarrassment to themselves.

As the light began to fade, we set off on our three-hundred and fifty mile journey to Paris. Our intention was to get away from Brittany. As we were now presumed dead, we had to be careful not to be seen by anyone who might inform the Resistance that we were still alive. Our plan was to go to Paris for a while and then proceed to north-eastern France where we would set up our escape route to Portugal.

Chapter Seventeen

We decided to head southeast, skirting Redon, and then head east past Le Mans and Chatres and on to Paris. We would follow the minor roads avoiding towns and would try to get lifts from passing farmers when ever possible. By doing this, we were able to travel part of the way in daylight.

When passing through built up areas we separated and took it in turns to enter shops, when it became necessary to buy food. Most nights we were able to find a shed or an open barn to shelter in. On several occasions whilst walking on the road, we had to slip into a ditch or hide behind a hedge as German patrols passed by. We had a few lifts from passing vehicles but there was always a chance of meeting up with a roadblock, so we were cautious when approaching or leaving a town and never stayed too long with any one person.

Finally, we arrived at the outskirts of Paris. We then split up, agreeing to meet at a café on the Boulevard Montparnasse where Pete would be able to make contact with Stephen in England. I acquired an old bicycle that someone had carelessly left outside a shop, and arrived at the café that evening. Pete had done even better. He had stolen an old van, which he had left parked two streets away from the Boulevard where we were meeting.

I went into the back room of the café. Pete was drinking a glass of wine and flirting with a very attractive French girl. 'Marçel, I've been in touch with Stephen. He's delighted to know that we are both dead. I also have a nice surprise for you. Gerda will be at the café Paradis at seven tomorrow night.'

My mind went back to Gerda's parting words—I was looking forward to meeting her again. I wondered if I really would go to bed with her.

'*Mirelle, Cherie*, untangle yourself from me and go and get us some food; we have not had a decent meal for the last two weeks.' Pete poured me a glass of red wine. 'This is Stephen's Paris office and where both Gerda and I are able to make contact with him. It's also a very safe house; even the Resistance don't know of its existence so there is little chance of the Germans ever finding it. However we have to be constantly on our guard, so always be extra careful when coming and going from here.'

Mirelle's father appeared with two large steaming bowls of '*soup d'onion*' and a basket of bread. 'Marçel, meet our good friend, Jean. He will be looking after you here for quite some time. I'm going off to organise the truck which we will be using to deliver our wine to northern Europe.'

Pete leaned back in his chair. 'The Allied invasion will take place at any time now which means there will be absolute chaos in Paris from then on. So be ready to move out as soon as I get back, and perhaps by then, our first clients will be ready to leave. Keep an eye on Gerda as I think she might have gone too far making contacts with the Germans.'

After our meal and second bottle of wine, Pete showed me to my room at the top of the building. It was an attic with a low ceiling and had a fantastic view of Paris. Pete went back downstairs and I collapsed on my double bed. When I woke up it was almost noon.

Down in the café they were serving lunch so I tucked into steamed trout and boiled potatoes. Pete had left so I took a walk along the Boulevard to the railway station, the Gare Maine Montparnasse. There was very little traffic on the roads but I noticed crowds of German soldiers waiting at the station. They were leaving Paris and heading for the coast.

At seven I found the café Paradis; it was in a side street just off the Rue d'Assas. Gerda was sitting at an outside table and I was shocked to see the change in her. She looked pale and drawn and had lost weight. Gerda had only been in Paris for six months but in that time she appeared to have aged at least ten years. When she saw me, she jumped up and ran towards me. We embraced. She hadn't lost her infectious laughter. 'Marçel dear, I am so pleased to see you.' The feeling was mutual. I held her in my arms and we kissed. 'Come, Marçel, I will show you my apartment. We have so much to talk about, I am so happy to see you again.'

I held her hand tightly. 'You are looking great Gerda. Paris must agree with you. It's good to be with you again.' That last bit I really meant.

Gerda's apartment was only a few streets away. It was a smart building and must have been built just a short time before the war. We climbed a wide staircase to the second floor and Gerda let me in to her delightful apartment. Her lounge room was large with a high ceiling. French windows led out to a small balcony. Her delicate furniture looked good with the polished floor and Afghanistan rugs. Gerda took off her coat. She had lost weight and now had an even more superb figure.

'You are looking so well, Marçel, in six months you have grown so big and strong and now I have you to protect me and perhaps who knows . . .'

We both curled up laughing. I could see the colour returning to her cheeks but I was waiting to hear what it was that had made her so stressed. 'What is it Gerda? What has happened to you in the last six months?'

'Dear boy, let us finish the champagne, what I have to say is not at all pleasant, I need to talk but it is hard to start and I don't want to spoil this moment.' Gerda emptied her glass and moved over to the window.

'In the last few months the most horrific truth of what is happening in the concentration camps has been revealed to me. Thousands of men, women and children are being killed every day. A relatively large number of the *Gestapo*, my people, are torturing and killing innocent people all over Europe in an effort to stamp out resistance and wipe out all the Jews. The German population stand by and do nothing, with all the bombing of our cities and living in constant fear from the *Gestapo*, they have been completely traumatised.'

'I have met some of these evil men, they are no longer human. When I talk to them I feel I am talking to men of ice. The coldness coming from them makes me shake not from fear but from absolute horror. They are no longer human beings but are creatures from hell.' Gerda paused. 'I will do everything in my power to help you to eliminate these creatures. They cannot be allowed to walk on this earth.' Her voice broke and there were tears in her eyes, a mixture of compassion and anger. I stayed silent to give her time to collect herself. Gerda shook herself, forced a smile and changed the subject.

'Marçel, very soon when the invasion of France starts, the Germans will withdraw from Paris and the French Resistance will take over. For a time there will be a period when they will punish the collaborators. There are many French people with scores to settle—some collaborators will be killed; both men and women. Already I have seen women beaten and their heads have been shaved. Believe me, the people in the Resistance will show no mercy to the girls that have given themselves to the enemy.'

Gerda filled her glass and took a long sip before continuing, 'I shall personally be in great danger until the Allies arrive. In order to collect a lot of the information that I have sent already back to London, I have had to mingle and even flirt with several German officers. They have also made several visits here to my apartment. This has not gone unnoticed. I believe I am a marked woman.' Gerda came behind me and put her hands on my shoulders. 'Once the liberating forces arrive I will be safe. I will be taken on to Germany where I can continue my work and be safe whilst working with the Allied Forces.'

I got up and put my arms around Gerda. 'It's obvious you are already in great danger, Gerda. From now on don't go anywhere without me. As soon as things turn really nasty you must come to our café and stay in my room. As you know, it's very safe there but you will have to stay indoors until the Allies arrive to take you away.'

Gerda took my hand. 'Dear Marçel, once again you come to my rescue my knight in armour. I still have much work to do but it will be good to know you are somewhere about when I have to go out into the streets. But come, Marçel, we still have lots of celebrating to do.'

Gerda led me to her bedroom—it really was a splendid double bed.

It was after midday when I made coffee and returned to find Gerda asleep again. She looked lovely lying there. Gerda was six years older than me, but in one night she had taught me how to make love. She was both gentle and passionate. I felt very warm towards her, we would always have a very special friendship, but no one could ever replace that one magical evening spent with Simone. That first love would always remain with me.

Later that afternoon we set out to explore Paris in the spring; we walked for miles holding hands and laughing. Even in those difficult days, Paris in spring was something extra special.

During the next few weeks, whenever Gerda was not working, we spent our time together. Some nights I stayed with her but many evenings she had to meet up with the

German officers. I tried not to feel jealous. I knew she hated having to play up to these often revolting men. I could see she was making herself a prime target and would soon be in great danger from the loyal French people.

We were walking through the Jardin Luxembourg one day, when Gerda told me that she had four clients for us, with two more likely to join them. They were all men who had worked in the death camps and wanted to get out of Germany whilst they could. I told her we expected them to pay five thousand US dollars or the equivalent in Swiss francs up front. She thought this quite reasonable and wanted to know if we would soon be ready to start our operation.

It was several weeks since I had heard from Pete. I expected him to turn up at any time. I wondered if he had found a suitable truck by now.

And then one day I heard gunshots coming from just a few streets away. Several German armoured cars went rushing by, after a while the shooting stopped. The next day we got the news—the Allied forces had landed in Normandy.

I went around to Gerda's apartment. I made her pack a bag and almost had to drag her over to the café. Once there, I managed to get a small room for her next to mine. Later I went back and collected all Gerda's paperwork and as many of her personal treasures as I could find.

Over the next few days we could hear sporadic fire coming from all directions. German vehicles were passing up and down the Boulevard all day. The firing continued at night. The Germans would stamp out one small group only to find they would start up again a few streets away.

Gerda wanted me to collect some of her books and a favourite painting, so I returned to the apartment to find it had been broken into. It had been looted and trashed. There was nothing left. I wondered what would have happened to Gerda if she had been there at the time.

A week later a heavy truck loaded with large wine casks arrived outside the café. Pete was back and ready for action.

It was a superb truck. It had been concealed on a farm throughout the Occupation and was in perfect condition. Pete had bought it on the black market through one of his many contacts. He had taken it to a remote repair garage in a small country town where he was able to convert it to suit our needs.

The truck had a canvass cover similar to the covers on the army trucks. Pete had got an old wine cask maker to attach three extra-long casks to the rear of the driver's compartment. Loose casks were always kept stacked in front of these casks. Behind the driver's seat there was a concealed trap door. A man could just squeeze through into one of the wine casks.

Once inside the cask, another trap door led through to the second cask and then on to the third cask. There was room in each cask for two men to stretch out or to sit up. The casks contained a mattress, pillow and blankets, water, a sealed can for toilet purposes, a container for food and a small electric light that ran off the truck's batteries. I was reminded of our hiding place on the barge.

In case of an accident, each cask had a concealed emergency escape panel on the top of the cask. At least that is what we told our clients! There was plenty of ventilation on the underside of the three casks, which was essential when travelling in hot weather especially in Spain and Portugal.

Extra fuel tanks, spare wheels and a water tank had been

fitted to the truck. Stephen's department in London had somehow managed to send over Portuguese number plates, registration and insurance papers, all stamped and legal. Pete and I now had Portuguese passports, which showed that we had recently arrived in France from Portugal via Spain. I was now Marçel Beaumont and Pete, Pierre Lonsdale. 'I'm pleased, Marçel, we have been able to retain our first names, it can become so confusing.'

The three of us sat around a table, Mirelle brought us a large bowl of *Pot-au Feu* and I explained to Pete the dangerous situation that Gerda was in and that her apartment had been raided and destroyed by the Resistance. I also told him that Gerda had possibly six clients ready and waiting to use our services.

'It would seem that it is time for the three of us to move out. We now have the transport and a legitimate business in neutral Portugal. I have taken over the lease of the property, which used to be the northern depot for the pre-war distribution of the Portuguese wines, so we now have a base to work from.' Pete had not wasted any time in the last few months. It looked as if we were now ready to start our real business.

'If we move to our depot, which is near to Colmar and only a few miles from the Rhine River, are you still able to make contact with those clients that are ready to travel, Gerda?'

I could see a distinct change in Gerda; she had come to life again and leaned forward eagerly. 'I am in direct contact with these people and furthermore they are just across the Rhine near the town of Freiburg. At present it would be easy for them to join us.'

Pete slapped the table. 'Well that's it, chaps! The sooner we get out of Paris the better. Gerda, you can be the official manageress of the depot until the district is liberated. You will be unknown there and no one will bother you. Marçel and I can make our first trip to Portugal where by now everything should be ready for us.'

We finished our meal. Pete asked Mirelle to close the café whilst we loaded the truck with all Gerda's gear, which we put in one of the casks. Pete and I kept our two bags in the cab of the truck. We stowed the Sten guns, pistols, hand grenades and explosives in another hidden container. This was concealed below the space under the passenger seats, which held all the tools for the truck. I went quietly back into the kitchen, wrapped a meat knife in a cloth (my faithful bayonet was still in England) and fastened it inside my trousers.

When all was ready we waited until no one was in sight. Gerda slipped quickly out of the café and climbed into the cab of the truck. She wriggled through the trap door and into the cask. I put my head through. 'Don't panic, Gerda, as soon as we are well clear of Paris we will let you out.'

We had about two hundred miles to travel so we decided to stop for the night before reaching the town of Nancy. The next morning would be an easy run to Neuf Brisach, which was close to our destination.

We were stopped twice on our way out of Paris. Our papers were checked and were found to be in order. At one place we had to make a detour as the road was blocked. We could hear guns firing; the Resistance men were shooting from some of the buildings nearby. The Germans were beginning to find themselves in an impossible situation, which would finally force them to withdraw from Paris.

At last, well clear of the city, we helped Gerda out from her, as she said, quite comfortable bed. Three very cheerful people sat in the cab of the truck singing bawdy songs, and for the moment forgetting all the horrors that they were to face in the months to come.

We stopped at an *auberge* just outside Nancy that also sold fuel. Pete had to pay black market prices for fuel that had been stolen from the Germans. We bought bread and some cheese from the *auberge* and moved on to a quiet parking spot near the main road. Pete decided to sleep in the cab where he was able keep a watch on the truck. Gerda and I cuddled up in one of the casks. I'm sure not many people can boast that they have made love in a wine cask!

Next morning we passed through Nancy without a problem Gerda stayed in the wine cask. At Colmar, we stopped at a factory that made equipment for wine producers and bought some new equipment, including a small conveyer system, which we would take back to Portugal for José.

Just outside of Colmar, we were stopped at a roadblock and searched. The officer in charge carefully studied our papers and passports. We explained that we were taking the equipment in the back of the truck to Portugal. 'I wish I could come with you. We will be lucky to survive the next few months.' He gave us back our papers and we continued on.

We stopped at Neuf Brisach where Pete collected some keys and soon after, arrived at our newly-acquired depot. I unlocked the gates and we drove into a yard. There were two large sheds on one side of the yard and a house on the other.

We parked the truck in one shed; the other larger shed was used for storing wine. Gerda scrambled out and joined us. 'You can now resume a normal life Gerda, your papers will cover you whilst you are here and you'll have no trouble from the Resistance. You are now the manageress of our French depot.'

An office took up most of the space in the front of the house, Pete had already had the power and the telephone connected and there were desks, filing cabinets and a typewriter. Although the place was in a mess, we soon cleaned it up. The previous occupiers must have left in a hurry.

The house was the same, it had been well furnished but there was a lot of work needed to make it habitable again. The three of us set to and a few days later, we had a comfortable home, an organised office, clean sheds and a tidy yard.

Gerda and Pete went to Colmar and returned with a stack of bits and pieces for the house and a good stock of food and wine. This was to be our second home.

Gerda had spent some time in the office and had made contact with our clients. We expected to meet up with them the following week.

We had decided that, for our own safety, there could not be a preliminary meeting with our clients. They had to be desperate enough to take us on trust, once committed; there would be no turning back for them.

We in our turn had to take the chance that their money might be forged. If at any time they became too difficult or attempted to turn back, we would have to kill them. This could be a problem for us as we would then have to dispose of all six of them before arriving at our vinery in Portugal.

Three days later, we arranged to pick up our clients at a quiet spot close to the Rhine River at five am. They would be crossing the Rhine in a small motor boat, which in itself was going to be very risky.

We guessed they must be paying a heavy bribe to someone

to bring them across. Crossing the Rhine without being detected would be extremely difficult unless they had the help of local authorities.

If they were seen and followed, we would then be at risk. We had to make sure that at the slightest hint of trouble we would be able to slip away undetected.

Chapter Eighteen

I was a cold misty morning when we met our clients at a disused sand pit close to the river. Pete had dropped me off two hours earlier. I had been watching the sand pit from a distance, to make sure only six people got off the motor boat, which had just crossed the Rhine.

I walked over towards the group. I had them covered with the Sten gun and was quite prepared to use it if it had turned out to be trap. I was joined by Pete and we approached this sorry group of men.

As instructed, they each carried a small suitcase and were all dressed in drab looking civilian clothes. I made them stand in line whilst Pete carefully searched each one, to make sure they were not carrying weapons. They became angry when Pete searched through all of the suitcases. Every suitcase contained a bag or box filled with gold, diamonds and valuable gems. Pete ignored this and handed back the cases to each of the men. There were no knives or guns.

Pete carefully explained to them that they would be travelling in the truck's hidden compartment by day, and would be allowed out for a short spell at night for exercise and food. The journey would take five days; they would then rest for a while before starting their long sea journey to Salvador. They were to make as little noise as possible. If they heard one hoot from the truck, they were to remain silent; two hoots would be the all clear. Anyone who made trouble on the journey would be jeopardising the safety of the whole group and the group would have to deal with that person themselves, or we would be forced to kill him.

We set off along a track that led out of the sandpit and turned up a side track, which soon became a footpath with high bushes on either side.

The truck was parked in a small clearing out of sight of the main road where we could have made our escape if things had gone badly wrong for us.

Pete gathered the Germans around him. 'You will enter the truck through the small trapdoor behind the driver's seat and you will pay me before you enter.' Pete pulled back the driver's seat and exposed the entrance to the barrels.

'There are three double beds, so select your partner carefully, as you will get to know each other intimately in the next few days. You will pay me as you enter the truck.' We showed them how to enter the casks with their cases. Pete collected their money as they climbed in. Thirty thousand dollars was a good start towards covering our costs.

We drove back to the depot and Pete gave Gerda the money.

She was to deposit it into our bank account in Switzerland, which was not far from where we were. We passed six food packs through the trap door to our clients. I gave Gerda a big hug and a kiss, I wished she could have joined us; said our farewells and set off.

Pete had already carefully planned our route, which cut across France using minor roads all the way to Bayonne, via Chalon, Limoges, crossing the Garonne River at Marmonde, then on to Bayonne.

We would cross the Spanish frontier at Hendaye, at San Sebastian we would then head south to Vitoria Gasteiz with a straight run across Spain via Salamanca, and then finally crossing into Portugal near Guarda and on to Aveiro' which was only just a short distance from our castle.

I was soon to realise how much organisation and work Pete had put into this route over the past months. Not only had he carefully worked out the route, which he had gone over several times, but he had also arranged the night stops, which would also be our fuelling depots.

At the end of each day we arrived at a secluded building. Sometimes it was an old farm house and at other times a deserted factory. Pete had gone to the trouble of leasing these buildings; they were always securely kept locked and were well away from habited buildings.

At each stopping place, there was a store of tinned food, blankets, spare mattresses and pillows, and a large stock of fuel. In France Pete had purchased quantities of fuel on the black market, in Spain and Portugal there was less of a problem, but he still made sure there was always a good reserve of fuel at our stopping points.

Pete and I took turns to drive, usually in four-hour shifts.

It was dark when we arrived at our first stop, which happened to be an old canning factory on the outskirts of Moulins. We drove into the yard and I locked the gates behind us.

Our clients climbed out of the casks and exercised themselves around the yard. We both kept a revolver in our belts, we did not want anyone straying off, and they had to stay in sight at all times.

I went into the locked storeroom, which Pete had equipped with everything we needed. There was a long table but no chairs. I found a primus stove and opened a few tins of soup. We had ample bread, which we had brought with us. Outside, Pete had made the clients bring out their toilet containers from the casks, which they then emptied and washed out ready for the next day.

We herded them into the storeroom where they helped themselves to the soup. I made some coffee whilst Pete and I waited for them to finish eating. We were most surprised how submissive they were, they must have realised that far from being the sadistic bullyboys, they were now dependant on us and that we had complete control over their destiny. They talked very little amongst themselves, they all had so much cruelty to account for in the last few years of their lives, any trust for each other had long gone.

I understood what Gerda had said, they seemed to exude evil. Their expressionless faces no longer appeared to be human, each one with his bag of blood money taken from their dead victims.

When they had all finished feeding themselves we let them walk around the yard for a short time, then herded them back into the casks. Pete fixed the lock on the trapdoor in case anyone decided to stray in the night.

We fed ourselves and cleaned up the storeroom, refuelled the truck and checked the water and oil. This was to be our routine for the next few nights. Pete slept in the cab and I climbed into the back of the truck. I was quite pleased with our first day, we had collected them without any problem and they had not given us any trouble so far.

At dawn we exercised the clients, gave them coffee and bread and were ready to set off on the next leg of the journey. We continued across France to Limoges without any problems. We saw very few Germans on the way; they were fully occupied in northern France by now.

Our next stop was at an old farm north of Bergerac. This was at a very quiet part of the country with no other properties in sight.

Our clients seemed to be suffering from the exhaust fumes; they were very quiet, and not interested in talking amongst themselves or in taking any exercise, so I applied a little pressure on them.

I remembered the circle of slave workers I had seen way back, when with other boys we had witnessed the beating of those starving men. I soon had them running in a circle and I stood in the middle of the circle, urging them on and on until I could see they were ready to drop, but I refrained from using a whip. To my surprise, they obeyed me without a murmur—they too seemed to be traumatised.

The next day was a much shorter run, so we left a bit later in the morning and drove a little slower, for our benefit as well as for our passengers.

A group of German soldiers were waiting at the bridge that crossed the river Garonne. I gave a single toot on the horn to warn our clients to keep quiet. Our papers were examined very carefully and our truck was searched for the first time by the *Feldgendamerie*. Much to our relief, we were told to continue on our way. As soon as we were well clear of the bridge, I gave the all clear with two toots on the horn much to the relief, I'm sure, of our six passengers.

We arrived at our last stop in France, a quite respectable house with a large shed at the back. We were able to park the truck in the shed for the night as well as being able to feed and exercise our clients.

Early the following morning, having warned our clients to be extra quiet that day, we set off for Hendaye where we were to cross into Spain. There were still a few Germans at the checkpoint but I wondered for how long. They would soon have to retreat to northern France or be cut off from Germany.

The Spanish officials seemed quite casual, we showed our papers and passports and quickly passed through the checkpoint. We now had a long run to Salamanca on very poor roads. It was well after midnight when we finally arrived at the farm just a few miles from Salamanca. Our clients were in a poor state when we let them out, but by the time I had finished exercising them, they had completely recovered and were ready for food.

I had stopped the truck and bought some supplies on the way, so I was able to cook a good meal. We opened some bottles of wine to restore everybody's spirits.

We were helping the clients back into the casks when I noticed a figure slipping away between the buildings. I picked up my knife and followed. I quickly ran around the back of the buildings until I was able to get ahead of him. I waited in a doorway. As he came level I grabbed him holding the knife at his neck, he froze, I was about to slit his throat, but I knew he was one of our clients, and we had much more fitting end for him.

'You were lucky this time my friend, don't try that again or your colleagues will tear you apart.' I led him back to the truck. Later I could hear thumping and some stifled moans coming from his cask.

The next day we had a much shorter run but we had to negotiate some very bad roads through very rough country. We crossed the border into Portugal, drove through the town of Guarda, and finally came down to the flat lands by the coast arriving at Aveiro. We were almost there.

It was late afternoon when we drove through the archway into the courtyard of our castle and José closed the gates behind us. We had made it.

We were all relieved to leave the truck, five of the guests looked quite cheerful as they descended, the sixth one was a mess. He had been well and truly 'done over' by his travelling companions!

José and Maria were at the front door to welcome us; the inside of the house had been redecorated and looked superb. Maria took our clients up stairs, they all seemed quite happy to share rooms—maybe having been locked up together in the casks for a few days they had become attracted to each other. All the showers were soon in use, thank goodness, after five days in the casks the Germans were in need of a good shower.

Maria and José were delighted that we were back. Pete declined Maria's promise of a celebration dinner that night. 'Maria, we will have a celebration party as soon as our guests have left.' José wanted to take us on a tour of inspection around the vinery but first we went out to the jetty to inspect the launch, which had been delivered the day before. Our launch had arrived at night and the crew had immediately boarded a second launch and left. We presumed they would be returning to England or possibly Gibraltar. Our yacht was a converted ex-Royal Navy motor launch. It had been painted white and all signs of any armament had been carefully removed. It was now a pleasure yacht.

In the large wheelhouse, on the chart table, we found the registration papers. The boat had been registered in Porto in our names and was fully insured. There was a letter from Stephen wishing us good luck and also, stating that we now owed his department just over half a million pounds.

The wheelhouse was fully equipped including a two-way radio, radar and safety equipment. On the chart table were charts of the Portuguese coastline, and the local waters.

Forward of the wheelhouse, there was a galley and a dining area and ahead of that, four double berth cabins and a bathroom. At the rear end, the stateroom had been converted into a lounge area, with leather-covered seats and a large polished table in the centre. There were no portholes, just a skylight that had a strong metal grill beneath it and which was firmly locked on the outside.

Back in the wheelhouse, I pressed the starters and the two powerful motors roared into life. We noticed a cloud of smoke coming from the exhaust outlets. Excellent.

We went back into the castle, well pleased with the launch. This was ideal for our purpose we had in mind.

We found Maria in the well-equipped kitchen, busy preparing the evening meal. We decided that our clients should eat first, and we would have our meal later when the Germans had gone to bed.

Having made sure all the staff had left for the night and all the exits from the castle were securely locked, we set off with José to inspect the vines.

A good part of the vinery had been cleared of weeds and the vines cut back, and already they were showing a healthy new growth. 'We still have a long way to go but by next season we will have all the vines back in production.' José was a happy man.

It was dark when we got back to the castle and Maria was serving the evening meal to the Germans. They just sat there silently stuffing themselves. I wondered what they were thinking, or were they now just brain-dead. Perhaps the horror of what they had been doing had finally caught up with them.

'Whilst you are here, gentlemen, you will have to stay in your rooms during the day. You can exercise out in the yard in the evening, when all the workers have gone home. On no account must you speak to any member of the staff whilst you are here—this is for your own safety. As soon as we get news as to when your cargo ship is due, our luxury motor-launch will take you out to your ship, and you will be on your way to South America. It could be tomorrow night.' Pete placed two bottles of wine on the table. 'In the meantime, gentlemen, we invite you to sample our excellent wine.'

Chapter Nineteen

The following morning Pete and I refuelled the motor-launch, José had ensured that we kept a good stock of fuel at the Castle. He had also bought us several fishing rods and tackle—this would be our reason for taking the launch out at night.

We concealed the Sten guns and revolvers onboard just in case things went wrong for us, but the last thing we wanted were bullet holes in the cabin.

I started the motors and we set out on a trial run to familiarise ourselves with the channel leading out to the ocean.

The two of us had no problem handling the boat and an hour later we headed out through the entrance, then gave the engines full throttle. The launch leapt forward. The waves were breaking over the bow and we were forced to slow down to a safe cruising speed.

We turned around and headed back to the Castle, well pleased with the performance of the launch. We would take our guests out to their final destination tonight.

We told the Germans to be ready to leave at ten pm as the freighter would be picking them up at one am.

At ten that evening they shuffled aboard clutching their suitcases. I led them down into the rear saloon. When they had settled down, I closed the door and joined Pete. The engines roared into life, we cast off and were on our way.

After a while, Pete went down to the saloon and opened several bottles of champagne. 'Gentlemen, we would like you all to take a last drink with us before you set off on your final journey.'

Pete left the saloon, closing the door behind him, quietly locking and bolting it.

Some time later when we were well clear of the entrance, Pete went down to the engine room and opened a valve. The exhaust fumes were diverted to the saloon through small holes in the floorboards under the table. Pete then went on to the deck and closed the two saloon ventilators.

Three hours later, we stopped the engines, opened the hatch and ventilators and shone a flashlight down into the saloon— they were all dead—six empty Champagne bottles and six very dead 'deserting rats.'

They had died in the same way that they had killed so many innocent Jewish families.

We spent the next hour removing the bodies. We carried them up on deck, slipped them into the weighted body bags, which Stephen had thoughtfully supplied us with. Without any ceremony, we dropped them one by one over the side of the boat and into the water.

After removing all the gold, diamonds and other gems, we put the suitcases into weighted bags and they joined their owners on the ocean bed.

We headed back to the coast. It was a calm night so we decided to try our hand at fishing—to my amazement we caught several good-size fish, later to be our breakfast.

It was dawn when we passed through the entrance and headed back to the castle—we had disposed of all our garbage.

That night we had our celebration dinner with José, Maria and Alfonso. As far as they knew, we had safely delivered our guests to a ship heading for South America.

Pete estimated we must have collected in excess of a million pounds in gold. Not bad for our first run.

My train was approaching the station. It was time to collect myself. The noisy boys had already left the train.

For the next three years, except for the period when the Allies invaded France from the South, Pete, Gerda and I made a number of journeys, many from Northern France to Portugal. We had some good and some bad runs with these wartime murderers. We were able to rid the world of a number of evil people. We also collected a vast amount of money.

We used a good part of this blood money to help some of the holocaust survivors start a new life in countries they had only dreamed about. Years later we were to lose most of what was left of our money on another venture—but that is another story. Many years later, we are still in the business of moving, and removing, people.

JERSEY
St. Helier

Manche

MANCHE

SAINT-MALO

BREST

SAINT-BRIEUC

Dinan

Evran   ST-Domineuc

Canal de Brest à Nantes

Hédé

QUIMPER

ST-Grégoire

PONTIVY

RENNES

Blavet

Rohan

St Nicolas
des Eaux

Josselin

Pont-Réan

Bourg des
Comptes

Pont-Augan

Malestroit

Vilaine

LORIENT

Guipry-Messa

Atlantic Ocean

VANNES

Vilaine

REDON

Arzal   La-Roche-Bernard

Canal de Brest à Nantes   Blain

ST-NAZAIRE   Sucé-sur-Erdre

TO NANTES

Best-selling titles by Kerry B. Collison

*Also available:
his fact-based
political thriller...*

ALSO BY
Richard Le Normand...

In 1947 Marcel, Peter and Gerda, working for a special branch of the secret service, run an escape route from Germany, through France and Spain, to their castle on the Portuguese coast. The clients are minor war criminals; each one carries a case of gold, stolen from their concentration camp victims.

Unbeknown to the escapees, on arrival at the castle these Nazis are taken out to sea by launch to a non-existent freighter, eliminated, and their gold recovered. This is their 'escape to death' ...

Karl, a distant relative and protégé of Adolph Hitler, hopes to revive the Nazi party and become the second führer of Germany. He arrives in Portugal from South America to find out what has happened to his colleagues and the gold.

Marçel, Helga and Gerda, having survived the motor accident that killed all the clients, arrive at the castle to find total carnage. Stephen, Marçel's boss, arrives from London to help, and to cover-up the operation.

So begins a cat and mouse game in which Karl tries to kidnap the girls and recover the gold. Mick, an Australian survivor of the Spanish civil war, becomes involved with his ketch and a classic battle between good and evil is played out on land and sea.

AVAILABLE FROM SID HARTA PUBLISHING